A MESSAGE FROM CHICKEN HOUSE

Set in Viking times, this exciting novel follows tough and resourceful Ylva on her quest to avenge her mother's death. Her journey is one of survival, spirit and pure drive – but it's also a story about learning to trust again, in spite of the wolves and raiders that fate sends against you . . . something that we all have to prepare for!

Danr Smior is the incredible Dan Smith's name in Old Norse, so I've decided to call him that from now on. Bravo, Danr – more thrilling stories like this, please!

BARRY CUNNINGHAM
Publisher
Chicken House

SHE WOLF

DAN SMITH

Chicken House

2 PALMER STREET,
FROME, SOMERSET
BA11 1DS

Text © Dan Smith 2019

First published in Great Britain in 2019
Chicken House
2 Palmer Street
Frome, Somerset BA11 1DS
United Kingdom
www.chickenhousebooks.com

Cover and interior design by Steve Wells
Cover illustration © Jill Calder
Typeset by Dorchester Typesetting Group Ltd
Printed and bound in Great Britain by CPI Group (UK) Ltd, Croydon, CR0 4YY

The paper used in this Chicken House book is made from
wood grown in sustainable forests.

1 3 5 7 9 10 8 6 4 2

British Library Cataloguing in Publication data available.

PB ISBN 978-1-910655-93-1
eISBN 978-1-912626-23-6

For Anisha and Ashwin.
Be kind. Be brave. Be strong.

Lindisfarena
Bebbanburg

Close-up map

Ylva arrives

Gyruum

Dunholm

Cetreht

Northumbria

Danes attack and occupy Eoforwic (Jorvik) Nov 866

Eoforwic

River Humber

The Great Heathen Army of Vikings arrives, 865

Snotengaham

Hreapandune

Mercia

East Anglia

Grantaceaster

Lundene

Cippanhamm

Wessex

Wiht

The Witch's Island

Seatun

NORTH SEA

Barghest Caves

Hand-shaped
Rock

The Trader's Hut

Ylva's Journey

December 866

Ylva
(eel-va)

1

The Three-Fingered Man

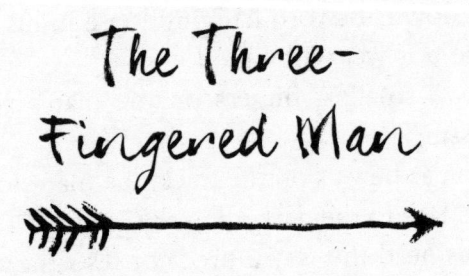

Ylva flinched when she heard Mother shout. It was unexpected, and the sound was so full of fear and pain, it took her a moment to realize what it was. A second shout told her she hadn't imagined the first, and when it cut short there was only silence from the hut.

Crouching in the snow-covered bracken at the edge of the forest, Ylva kept her arm around her dog, Geri, and stared across the track at the lopsided door of the trader's hut. Her fingers tightened around the leather-bound handle of her axe, hard enough to make her knuckles pop.

Trees creaked and cried in the wind that flooded the mountainside.

When the door opened, a bald and bearded giant of a man emerged and stepped down into the deep snow that lay on the track. As tall and wide as two ordinary men, he had blue-tattooed runes arched over each ear, and a history of past battles etched in scars on his face. Rings of black kohl were painted around the palest blue eyes, making them fade into his skull like the eyes of the dead. A Viking raider, Ylva thought, probably from the same shores she had sailed from. Dressed in grey wolf furs, he moved slowly like a beast, walking with his head down, a sword hanging loose in his left hand. The blade was wet with blood.

The two smallest fingers on the man's right hand were missing.

As soon as he was on the track, the man stopped and raised his face to the darkening sky. He sniffed hard and turned his head the way a predator tests the air for the scent of its prey.

Instinctively, Ylva pulled Geri down so she and the elkhound were lying flat on their bellies, side by side. The snow was perishing and her insides flushed ice-cold as the man on the track opened his mouth and tasted the breeze. There was a flicker in his pale eyes, and his lip curled ever so slightly at one side.

'You smell something?' A woman appeared from the hut behind him. She was tall and strong, with braided hair the colour of burning winter sunsets.

'Can't be sure.' The man's voice was the rumble of wagon wheels over wood.

The flame-haired woman twisted a necklace around the knuckles of her right hand; the same necklace Mother had been wearing when she had entered the hut. Nothing more than a leather cord and a small, wooden coin-shaped locket. It was simple. Worthless to anyone other than Ylva.

'I don't smell anything.' The woman lifted her nose to the freezing air. 'You're just—Wait.' She put the necklace over her head and stepped down on to the track. She drew a short sword from the folds of her furs and peered into the trees.

Geri squirmed as if he wanted to make a run at the woman – like a fox pouncing from a tuft of grass to catch a rabbit. But this woman was no startled rabbit, so Ylva pressed him to the ground and wished they could become part of it. She held his mouth closed to stop him from making a noise, and let the deep snow cocoon them. Ylva took tiny sips of air, afraid the steam of her breath would give them away. She dared to lift her head only just enough to see over the top of the icy crust.

The woman stalked across the track and stopped at the treeline. She scanned left and right, then stared ahead, as if she were looking directly at Ylva and Geri, half-buried in the snow. 'You're right,' she said. 'I smell it too.'

She took a step towards the bracken, hair shining in the last of the day's light, but stopped when a wolf howled in the mountains behind the hut. The haunting cry echoed in the dusk, and the woman paused with her boot mid-step. Her eyes narrowed and she glanced over her shoulder at the man.

'Let's move,' he said.

Her foot pulled back and the woman returned to the track. She stood for a moment, peering into the dark forest.

'The day's wasting.' The man flicked his sword hard, sending a spray of red across the crisp snow. He wiped the blade on his breeches, then jammed it into its scabbard and went to where his horse was hitched. Raven-black, with a long mane, and a shaggy coat, the animal's legs were thick and its back was wide. It must have been the only horse strong enough to carry such a giant of a man. Perhaps the biggest horse in all of Midgard – certainly the biggest Ylva had ever seen. Right then, she believed only Odin's mighty horse Sleipnir could be bigger.

The three-fingered man swung up into the saddle and waited for the woman to mount up. When they were both on horseback, they reached into the collars of their furs to pull scarves over their mouths as they looked back at the trees where Ylva and Geri were hiding.

With their noses and mouths covered, all that was visible of the raiders' faces was their kohl-lined eyes. But there was a clear white design painted on each black scarf; the bottom half of a skull. Upper and lower jaws. Teeth. And even from beneath the bracken, Ylva saw that the incisors were long, like a wolf's.

For a moment, she was watching monsters and she wanted to scream. But she didn't dare move. She *couldn't* move.

All she could do was bite the inside of her cheek and lie paralysed beside Geri as the two Vikings finally turned and rode away, the shields on their backs like eyes watching her. And in the centre of each black shield was the same painted design; a wolf skull.

2

Gods and Tears

─────────➤

Ylva stayed in the snow for a long time watching the riders disappear into the dusk. And even then, she waited as the night closed in and more snow settled. It fell in a dream, soft flakes as big as goose down, and she lay with one hand in Geri's thick black and grey fur, trembling in the cold as the snow began to bury them. Ylva wondered if they should stay there to die. They could disappear and be nothing.

But that wasn't what Mother had taught her, so she forced herself to stand and adjust her scarf and cloak. Geri stood beside her, almost tall enough to reach Ylva's waist. He was strong and well muscled, with a wolf-like coat and a tightly curled tail. When he opened his mouth and looked up at his friend, he displayed a good set of white teeth.

Ylva placed her hand on his head. 'We need to get inside.'

She crept from the trees and headed for the trader's hut, but halfway across the track, Geri stopped. He clamped his mouth shut and whined.

Ylva looked back at him. 'You're afraid,' she said.

Geri flattened his ears and took a step backwards as he stared at the lopsided door in front of them. He whined again, the grief-stricken sound echoing in the emptiness of the mountainside.

'No crying.' Ylva went to crouch in front of him. 'I need you now more than ever. Help me be strong.' She put her hand against one side of his head, and her face against the other. The smell of his fur was the most comforting smell in the world. 'We're warriors now.' Ylva spoke in his ear. 'Vikings. And we do whatever we must to survive. That's what Mother would say.'

Ylva knew Mother would be dead inside the hut, but she didn't allow herself to cry. Not now.

'Tears aren't a sign of weakness.' She made her voice firm when she spoke to Geri. 'But there's a right time for tears, and there's a wrong time. For us, survival always comes first; we do whatever it takes to survive. We have to remember Mother's words. Survival always comes first.'

She stood and looked down at him. 'Follow me.' She put one boot in front of the other until she reached the lopsided door, and when she pushed it open, she stepped in, with Geri at her heel. They stood for a while as she waited for her eyes to grow accustomed to the darkness, Ylva touching Geri's fur with the fingertips of one hand, her axe held tight in the other.

At the far end of the hut was a rough wooden counter. To the right, close to a firepit, two basic square tables stood with chairs tucked underneath. A fire crackled in the pit, providing poor light, and warming the flame-blackened pot that hung over it on a tripod. The smell of soup mingled with the scent of earth and fire and sweat.

On the wall to the left, all manner of things hung on rusty nails – from horse tack to pots to strange tools and unrecognizable pieces of iron. Nothing that was of use to her. Piles of folded rugs and furs rested on crude shelves of splintered wood, and the dirt floor was crowded with chests of grain and smoked meat and fish.

For Mother, there was no dignity in death. She was lying face down near the grain chests with her hair splayed like freshly cut straw. Around her, the dirt floor was thick with blood.

Another body, a man, was lying against the counter at the back of the room.

Geri crossed the room to where Mother lay. He sniffed her, nuzzling at her neck and whining.

'No crying. Remember what Mother said. There's a time for tears, but this isn't it. This isn't the time.'

He stopped immediately, and lay down beside Mother. He watched Ylva with sad, dark-brown eyes. The two of them stared at one another for a long while before Geri finally relaxed and rested his chin on his large paws.

'Good.' Ylva closed the door.

With a grunt of effort, she lifted the drop-bar into place, checked the door was secure, and shrugged off her satchel. She slipped the axe into her belt and moved deeper into the room, hardening herself for what she had to do. A numbing emptiness filled the hut. It threatened to overwhelm her, but Ylva was strong. She was from a hard land and she had seen hard times. She had sailed across the sea, she had a bearded axe in her belt, and that made her a Viking.

'Survival always comes first,' she whispered as she pushed her heartache to the darkest place in her soul. She crouched beside Mother and put her hands underneath the motionless body. It took some effort to roll Mother on to her back, then Ylva rested, breathing heavily as she stared at the face she loved.

Geri watched her with questioning eyes, as if he were asking, *Is she really dead?*

'Yes.' There was no point putting an ear to Mother's chest to listen for a heartbeat. 'She really is.' Instead, Ylva arranged Mother's scarf and tidied her hair. She tried not to think of the times Mother had brushed hers, sitting by the fire, humming a tune. When she was finished brushing, she'd kneel in front of Ylva and tell her, 'Your hair is winter wheat, and your eyes are deepest summer.'

But she would never say those words again.

Ylva chewed her lip and slipped her hands into Mother's cloak, looking for her knife, but it was missing.

What about him? Geri glanced over at the man slumped dead against the counter.

'The trader, I suppose; the owner of the hut.'

Is he dead too?

'Yes, he's dead too.'

After a long moment to collect her thoughts, Ylva

took her knife from its sheath and cut a lock of Mother's hair. She carefully tucked it into a pouch tied to her belt before taking a blanket from the shelf and spreading it over Mother. When that was done, she went to the table by the firepit, pulled out a chair, and sat down.

She clicked her tongue and Geri came to sit by her side. Ylva leant over to hug him. She pressed her face against his fur and breathed his familiar scent of woodsmoke and fresh air. His fur had always smelt like that, and it had always comforted her.

'What have we done to anger the gods?' she asked. 'What have we done to make them abandon us?'

3

Niflheim

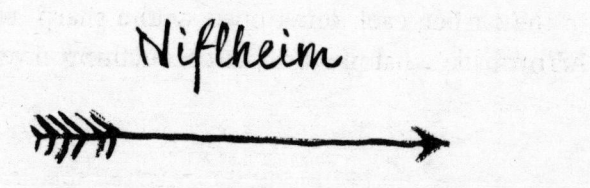

The logs in the firepit burnt down to nothing and the heat faded.

The night was as cold as a grave in the ice-world Niflheim, and the hut was the only place Ylva had seen in days. It was possible that the three-fingered man might return for warmth and shelter. Ylva couldn't waste any more time; she had to make sure they were safe.

Survival always comes first.

'Stay here.' She placed fresh wood on the fire, and Geri watched her go to the door. After rattling it several times to be certain it was secure, Ylva crossed the room, avoiding looking in Mother's direction. She got down on her knees to search the trader but found nothing useful. Behind the counter, though, she saw something lying on the floor in the damp dust.

She picked up the bow and turned it this way and that. There was strength and power in the wood, and though it was made for an adult, her small hand fit well in the grip. The weapon gave her mixed feelings of comfort and fear. It was an instrument of survival, and an instrument of death. An instrument of revenge. It was no coincidence to find it there.

'The gods put it here for me,' she told Geri. 'Maybe even Thor himself left it here as a sign.' As if to confirm that thought, there was a quiver full of arrows leaning in the corner, each one tipped with a sharp iron point. Arrows like that would pierce anything. Even a coat of mail.

One. Two. Three. Four . . . Her fingers brushed across the feathered fletchings as she counted the arrows over and over until she was sure how many there were. One. Two. Three. Four. Five . . .

Nine arrows. Nine sharp iron tips.

She rubbed the place where her collar chafed her neck as she looked across at the shape that was Mother beneath the blanket. Geri sat patiently by the table.

'I know what I have to do with these,' Ylva said.

Ylva placed the bow and the quiver of arrows on the counter and ignored Geri's questioning looks as she continued to search the hut, checking every corner and scanning every shelf. Anything useful and small enough to carry went in a line on the counter. Among other things, there was a bone-handled knife, and a clay pot containing charcloth and flint. There was salted fish, dried meat, and a small pouch of henbane seeds. She counted and checked everything twice – then once again, just to be sure – and stuffed it into the leather satchel she had taken from the body of a dead man several days ago. He had been one of many lying in the crimson surf beside the smouldering skeleton of a longship.

Soon, the satchel contained enough food and provisions to last a week, maybe two. The pouch of seeds was fastened for safekeeping beside the water bag on her belt, and the knife was tucked in beside it where it would always be in reach.

She rolled a blanket into a tight bundle, tied it with twine found on a shelf, and left it by the door along with her satchel. It would be easy to grab if she needed to make a quick escape. But for now, she wasn't going anywhere; it was warmer and safer in the trader's hut than it would be out in the forest, and there was the small comfort of hot soup bubbling over the fire.

The soup smelt bad, and the knots of gristle floating among the potatoes and carrots looked disgusting, but Ylva didn't know when her next meal might be, so she filled a clay bowl and sat by the fire with hot soup and a chunk of dry bread.

The powerful bow lay on the table in front of her, one arrow ready beside it, the others in the quiver close by.

Ylva didn't feel like eating, but she had to keep warm and strong, so she slurped the soup and watched Geri lying at her feet. He looked up at her, eyebrows twitching, and let out a quiet whine.

What do we do now? Where do we go?

'There's only one thing for us to do,' she told him. 'At first light, I'll bury Mother in the forest behind the hut.'

The ground will be hard. Cremation is a better way to send her to the gods.

'But if I build a pyre, the smoke will attract attention,' Ylva said. 'So I'll break the ground and bury her. And when she's buried, we'll track the three-fingered man. When we find him, I'll kill him.'

Geri put his chin on his paws. He licked his lips and sighed. *Why?*

'Because that's the way things work. It's what the gods expect.'

4

Young Wolf

Ylva faced the door and watched the shadows thrown from the firepit. She tried to stay awake but eventually her eyes closed to a troubled half-sleep of broken dreams. There was no way to know how long she slept, but it was still dark when Geri's growling woke her.

There was a second of confusion as she remembered where she was, then she jumped to her feet with the bow in one hand, an arrow in the other.

Geri was standing alert by the table, with his eyes fixed on the door, and his ears pricked forward.

'What is it?' Ylva asked. 'What did you hear?' She stood as still as a stone, and tilted her head to concentrate. The wind clawed at the walls of the hut. Trees wept and groaned in the forest. But when the wind dropped for a moment, it was just long enough for a soft sound to fill the emptiness.

Thump. Thump. Thump.

'What is that?'

Thump. Thump. Thump.

The slow and muffled thump of hooves on the snow-covered track.

Geri looked back at Ylva. *Someone's coming.*

With that terrifying thought, Ylva grabbed Geri by the scruff of his neck and dragged him across the hut. Jumping over the trader's body and backing away to the far corner behind the counter, she pulled two spare arrows from the quiver. She placed them within easy reach on the countertop, then put a third to the string of the bow.

'Stay out of sight,' she whispered to Geri.

The wind moaned like the dead rising from their graves. Heavy snowflakes pattered against the roof. Ylva's heart quickened. There was a mutter of a voice in the storm, and a moment later, the door rattled.

'Hey!'

The door rattled again, and a second later, an eye appeared at a gap in the shuttered window. The woman raised her voice and banged a fist on the wall.

Geri's muscles tightened and he lifted his lips to bare his teeth. He growled, long and deep, until Ylva hushed him and crouched lower, moving into the darkest shadows to keep out of sight. Holding the bow drawn and ready to shoot, she tried to give Geri a reassuring smile, but the shutter smashed inwards with an alarming crash. Ylva flinched as splinters and snow showered into the hut.

Before there was time to blink, a hand came through the broken shutter, reaching across to feel for the drop-bar. There was a thud as the heavy piece of wood fell to the floor, and the hand withdrew.

When the door swung open a single figure stood on the porch. The woman's mop of wiry black and grey hair, and the thick scarf pulled over her mouth gave her the look of a mean old bear that had lumbered out of the forest. Light from the fire glinted in her dark eyes. She carried a bag over one shoulder, and a short sword in her right hand.

The wind blew around her, bringing snow into the hut.

Ylva told Geri to stay where he was. She stood straight and drew the bow. 'Stop right there or I'll kill you.' She spoke the words loud and clear. She didn't let her voice waver.

The woman paused on the threshold and squinted into the darkness beyond the firepit.

'I mean it.' Ylva remained behind the counter but took a step forward out of the shadows so the woman could see the arrow aimed at her heart.

'Oh.' The woman leant her sword against the wall and raised her hands to show they were empty. She pulled her scarf away from her mouth as she glanced around the room, then looked at Ylva and softened her expression. 'A child? Please. Don't kill me. I'm sorry if I scared you.'

It was strange, the way the woman spoke. She used the same words Ylva would use, but they sounded different in her mouth. It reminded Ylva that she was foreign in this land.

'Really, child, don't be afraid,' said the woman. 'I'm not here to hurt you. I just want to get out of the cold, find somewhere warm.'

'I'm not afraid.' Ylva lowered her chin, trying to sound older than she was. 'And I'm not a child. If you try to come in here, I'll shoot you dead.' She flicked her gaze down to look at Geri crouched by her feet, then back up at the woman again.

'Huh, well, I'm afraid,' the woman said. 'I'm afraid of what's here in the dark, and what's out there in the forest. I'm afraid of freezing to death, too, because if I stay out here any longer, my blood's going to turn to ice, and I really don't want that.'

'Find somewhere else.'

'There is nowhere else. And you're making me nervous pointing that thing at me, so I'd prefer you to point it somewhere else.'

'I know how to shoot and I know how to shoot fast,' Ylva said. 'Don't think I won't do it. I'll kill you as easily as I'd kill a rat.'

'I don't doubt it,' the woman replied with a half-smile. 'I can see the wolf in you.' She held Ylva's gaze for a moment, then shifted her eyes to take in the state of the room. She let out a long deep sigh as she looked at Ylva once more. 'It's getting colder out here, and there's things I'd rather not run into. I really need to come inside.'

'So you can try to kill me?'

'Why would I do that?'

'Because you're a Saxon and—'

'You're a Dane?' The woman took a deep breath and puffed her cheeks as she let it out. 'Well, I don't care much about Vikings and Saxons and all that. People are people as far as I'm concerned, and every one of them deserves to be left in peace to live the life they want. And right now I'd very much like to come inside, and I'd rather do it without getting hurt. Will you promise not to put an arrow in me?'

Ylva didn't reply.

'Maybe we need an introduction,' the woman said. 'My name is Cathryn. I get by trading this and that, getting into trouble from time to time. How about you, young wolf? Do you have a name?'

Ylva kept the bowstring drawn back. 'I don't care to share it with you.'

Cathryn raised her eyebrows and nodded. 'Huh, well, I see. But I have to call you something. You're a fierce creature; how about Young Wolf?'

Ylva said nothing.

'Young Wolf it is then. Introductions made. And now we're not strangers any more, I think it would be proper for you to invite me inside to warm myself by the fire.' She smiled. 'Maybe even share some of what's cooking in that pot.'

Geri leapt up to put his front paws on the counter beside Ylva and look over at the wild woman. He was no longer agitated. He had stopped growling, his muscles were relaxed, and his breathing was normal.

'You think she's friendly?' Ylva whispered to him. 'That we should let her in?'

She has kind eyes. I like the look of her.

'You like the look of her?' Ylva stared into the woman's eyes, searching for the kindness Geri saw. 'You're sure?' Perhaps he was right; maybe this woman wasn't a threat. Even so, they would have to be wary of her. 'All right.' She raised her voice. 'You can come in.'

'Thank you.' Cathryn looked puzzled by Ylva's behaviour, but gave a small nod. 'And thank you for not killing me.' She dropped her bag beside Ylva's satchel. 'Now I don't want you getting worked up any more than you already are,' Cathryn said. 'But you should know I'm not alone.'

When she said it, a dark-skinned, dark-haired boy stepped out from behind her and showed himself. He was a few inches taller than Ylva, lean and dressed in a leather tunic and breeches. He wore a fur cloak over his shoulders, and fur-bound leather boots on his feet. A smooth, thick scar curved around his throat, as if he were wearing a necklace. He carried a bow in his left hand.

'This is Bron,' Cathryn said. 'He doesn't talk much, but what he lacks in talking he makes up for in scowling.' And with that, she used the heel of her boot to kick the door closed behind her.

Revenge

5

A Long Way from Home

⟫———————⟫

'It's treacherous out there.' Cathryn ran a hand through her thick curls, then rubbed life back into her face. 'Huh.' She wiped her eyes and looked around the room. 'Uh-huh.'

Once she had taken it all in, her gaze fell on Ylva, who was still half-hidden behind the counter. 'How old are you, child? My guess is a few years younger than Bron.' She gestured at the boy. 'Thirteen? You look about thirteen to me.' As she spoke, she put the drop-bar across the door and did her best to close the broken shutter, dampening the howl of the wind. 'And you're a Dane – in a part of Northumbria still controlled by Saxons. I'd say you're a long way from home.'

The boy had the presence of an animal coiled and waiting to strike; he remained by the door, watching

Ylva with dark and suspicious eyes. He held his bow loose in his hand.

'What are you doing this far north, child? Are you lost?' Cathryn finished with the shutter and faced Ylva as she waited for an answer. When Ylva didn't give one, Cathryn shrugged. 'And who's that lying by your feet? Is he the owner of this hut? You want to tell me what happened to him?'

'I didn't kill him,' Ylva said.

'That's not what I asked. But since you mentioned it, he doesn't look like he's asleep down there, so I'm guessing someone *did* kill him. And if it wasn't you, then who was it?' She rubbed her hands together and went to the shape hidden under the blanket on the floor. 'And who's this?' She bent down and took hold of one corner.

'Don't touch that,' Ylva warned.

'I have to see.' Cathryn lifted the blanket just enough to glimpse underneath. 'You know her?'

Ylva nodded once.

'This is your mother and—?'

'Yes, so don't touch.'

Cathryn sighed and lowered the corner of the blanket. 'I'm sorry.' She went to the pot over the fire and filled three clay bowls with soup before taking them to the table. With her foot, she pushed out a chair and pointed at it. 'Bron, come and sit down. You're scaring the poor child.'

The boy made a strange gesture with his right hand. He held a fist close to his hip and opened it suddenly as if he were throwing something aside. He kept his eyes on Ylva while he did it, and she stared right back at him.

'He's as wary of you as you are of him,' Cathryn said. 'And that's his way of saying "no". He doesn't speak much so he uses his hands.' She turned to Bron. 'Sit. Can't you see she's not going to hurt anyone?'

'Don't be too sure of that.' Ylva scowled. 'I'm even more dangerous than I look.'

'Oh really?' Cathryn said. 'Even more dangerous? Then I'll have to be careful what I say. Bron, sit down.'

Without taking his eyes off Ylva, the boy sighed and stalked across to the table where he took the chair Cathryn had pushed out for him. He leant the bow beside him and sat so he could watch Ylva from the corner of his eye.

Cathryn sipped the soup and coughed. 'Ugh, that's disgusting. Did you make this?'

'No. Why is his skin so dark?' Ylva asked.

Cathryn wiped her mouth with her hand. 'You mean Bron?'

'Yes.'

Cathryn grimaced as she tried the soup again. 'His ancestors lived in a place where it never snows and the sun shines from dawn to dusk. A place where everyone has dark skin.'

'I've never heard of such a place.'

'That doesn't mean it doesn't exist. It's a long way south of here, across the sea.'

'And why do you speak so strange? Do all Saxons speak like this?'

'So many questions,' Cathryn replied. 'Yes, all Saxons speak like this. Now you tell me something – what are you doing alone in a hut with dead people? What happened here?'

Ylva glanced at Geri beside her, his front paws still on the counter, and Geri looked back at her. *Tell them,* he seemed to say, and Ylva wondered why he trusted the woman. But he had always been a much better judge of character than she was.

Tell them.

'All right.' She nodded to him and turned her attention back to Cathryn. 'It was a man and a woman. I was outside. Mother came in to make a trade and . . .' Ylva's gaze settled on the blanket in the middle of the floor and her words caught in her throat.

'Huh.' Cathryn nodded without looking around. 'Just to trade? Nothing more than that? Are you sure she didn't come in here for another reason?'

'What other reason?' Ylva put a hand to her neck and touched her scarf.

'Don't get angry, child, I'm only asking if you could think of anything. It's just that if I was out there in the cold with my child and I had nothing to my name, no silver in my pocket, and I saw a warm hut with food inside, and I had a knife in my hand . . . I don't think anyone would blame a mother for trying to protect her child.'

'Who said we had nothing to our name? Mother had silver to trade. Lots of it. Why would I lie? Are you calling me a liar?'

Cathryn held up a hand. 'I'm calling you nothing of the sort. I can see you're an honest girl. Honest and dangerous.'

'Yes I am.'

Cathryn slurped her soup. 'So . . . you were telling me what happened.'

'Mother *did* have a knife as it happens – a good one – and silver to trade for blankets and a hot meal, so she—' Ylva bit the inside of her cheek and took a deep breath. 'Mother told me to wait outside while she went in. But then the man and woman came on horses.'

'A man and a woman?' Cathryn paused with her soup bowl touching her lips. 'On horseback?'

'Vikings. They went inside and . . . and when they came out . . .' Ylva bit her cheek hard enough to draw blood. This was not the time for crying.

'You sure they were Vikings?'

Ylva focused on turning her despair into rage. 'Of course. I know what Viking raiders look like. The way they were dressed, their weapons. They had shields with wolf skulls on them.'

'Wolf skulls? And when did they leave? Was it long ago?'

'Before dark.'

Cathryn looked across the table at Bron and they shared a concerned glance before she turned to Ylva. 'You didn't tell me why you're so far north. Ivar the Boneless took Eoforwic last month and most of the kingdom to the south now belongs to Vikings, but not here. We don't see many Danes in this area except the odd raiding party like the one that . . .' Her words trailed away as her eyes went to the shape on the floor. Her voice softened. 'A day's ride south of here we saw a burnt longship on the beach. There were bodies and . . . is that something to do with you?'

'I don't want to answer any more questions,' Ylva said.

'I understand.' Cathryn forced a smile. 'So why don't you come and sit down? The soup tastes like horse dung and slugs, but at least it's hot. It'll make you feel better.'

'Nothing will make me feel better. And I don't know you, so I don't trust you. Mother taught me not to trust anyone on the road. Survival always comes first.'

'Sounds like she was a wise woman,' Cathryn said. 'I might have liked her. But did she remember to tell you that sometimes you have to trust someone? That one day your survival might depend on it?'

'I trusted her.'

'But she's gone, so who will you trust now?'

'Myself,' Ylva said without hesitation. 'And the gods.'

'The gods? Really?'

'They're testing me,' Ylva said.

'Ah, I see. A test. Yes, that's the kind of thing your gods do, isn't it?'

'Because they want to make us strong. People say you Saxons only have one god, and that he's soft and weak. Is that true?'

'Sometimes softness is strength, child.'

Ylva looked confused. 'I don't understand.'

'You've never seen a blade of grass bend to the wind?' Cathryn asked.

'Grass and gods are different. You can't compare them.'

Cathryn smiled. 'You might be right. But have you considered that Bron and I might be part of the test you speak of? I mean, we're definitely not leaving, so we must have a part to play.' Cathryn sucked at her soup bowl again. 'And you can't stay behind the counter all night. I promise we don't want to hurt you, so you might as well join us here, close to the fire. The worst thing that'll happen is that your mouth will be assaulted by the taste of this disgusting soup.'

Ylva was sure she could stay behind the counter all night if she wanted to, but Geri had other ideas. The way his deep-brown eyes were fixed on her, his head tilted to one side, she knew what he would say if he could speak.

It's cold back here. I don't like it. We should be by the fire, where it's warm.

'We're staying where we are,' Ylva whispered. 'I don't trust them.'

But maybe she's right; maybe she is part of the test. And it's warmer over there. And there's hot food.

'No.' Ylva shook her head.

I don't want to be alone.

'All right.' Ylva grabbed the arrows and stepped away from the counter. 'But don't take your eyes off them.' She came towards the fire but didn't sit at the table with the strangers. She moved to the other table and pulled out a chair to sit facing them. Pleased to be back in the warmest part of the hut, Geri settled on the floor at Ylva's feet. He yawned, licked his lips, then rested his chin on his paws and closed his eyes.

Ylva wasn't quite so trusting. She placed the bow on the tabletop and laid both hands on it, ready to use it at a moment's notice. She watched the strangers through the fine strands of hair that fell across her face.

'You really know how to use that?' Cathryn pointed at the weapon.

'Yes.'

'And would you recognize the people who did this terrible thing to you?'

'Yes.'

'Huh.' Cathryn rubbed the tiredness from her eyes. 'You know . . . what happened to you is a horrible thing. If something like that happened to me, and I had a weapon like that, I'd feel as if it was begging to be used. If I was a Dane, with your gods, I might even tell myself it was destiny.' She looked up at the ceiling. 'That the gods had put the weapon in my hands.' She lowered her eyes to watch Ylva once more. 'Knowing what little I know of you, fierce child, I'd say you're planning to hunt the people who killed your mother. You want to make them pay for what they did because that's the Viking way, isn't it? You want revenge.'

Ylva stared at Cathryn.

'I know I'm right.' Cathryn picked up her bowl. 'One of the benefits of having lived as long as I have is that occasionally I'm right about something.' Steam rolled around her head as she drained the last of her soup. 'Ugh.' She pulled a face at the grim taste, and wiped her mouth. 'I don't usually offer advice, and almost never take it, but you should know that revenge is a sly beast. Holding something as dark as that in your heart is like grabbing Jormungandr the World Serpent by the tail – it's likely to turn around and swallow you whole . . . or spit poison in your face and let you suffer. Nothing will bring them back, Young Wolf. Not even revenge.' She looked over at the shape beneath the blanket. 'The best thing you can do is bite down on your pain and wait for it to soften. What's gone is gone, and there's no way to bring it back.'

6

Shield-Maiden

athryn kept her fur cloak on until the fire had warmed her through. When she shrugged it off on to the back of her chair, she revealed a tough leather tunic beneath. Across her stomach, she carried a knife big enough to skin a bear, and from one side of her belt hung a short-handled axe. Together with the sword she had left by the door, Cathryn was more than well armed.

She had told Ylva that she got by 'trading this and that', but Ylva was certain Cathryn wasn't a trader. The way she was dressed, the weapons she carried, she looked more like a warrior. A shield-maiden. Swords were expensive and difficult to forge, and the only people who owned them were those rich enough to have one made, or those who took them from the dead fingers of a defeated enemy.

Cathryn didn't look like a rich woman.

Bron hadn't spoken a word since entering the hut. He communicated with Cathryn using his hand-speak, making signs and gestures in the air, but he kept his eyes on Ylva. He watched her like a hawk watches the forest from above.

The night limped on and they each stayed in their seats, not speaking much at first, and then not at all.

Eventually Cathryn fell asleep sitting upright in the chair, and as soon as she started snoring, Bron's frown deepened further. He rolled his eyes at Ylva, as if the sound annoyed him, then went to the far side of the room where he took two blankets from the shelf and spread them on the dirt floor close to the fire. Satisfied with his makeshift bed, he lay down on it, hugged his fur cloak around his shoulders, and closed his eyes.

As she sat listening to Cathryn's snoring, and watching her enormous chest rising and falling, Ylva wondered if the woman might help her find the three-fingered man.

Or take us somewhere safe. Geri sat up and nuzzled Ylva for attention. He pressed his nose against her arm and lifted a paw on to her knee.

'Maybe,' Ylva whispered as she stroked the soft fur between his ears. 'Maybe. But I don't like the look of that boy. I don't like the way he watches me.'

Geri opened his mouth, letting his tongue loll out to one side. *You're afraid of him?*

'Of course I'm not afraid of him.' She leant down to

put her face against Geri's neck. 'I just don't like the look of him. He concerns me.'

Just after midnight, Ylva quietly pushed back her chair to stand and stretch her legs. She edged around the table, taking tiny steps so her boots wouldn't scuff the floor, and went to where Mother lay beneath the blanket.

She sank to the floor beside the body and sat with her legs crossed, placing the bow within easy reach. Geri sighed and curled himself beside her.

'Tomorrow will be the first of many long days,' Ylva said as she stroked his fur. 'I'll need you to watch over me.'

She glanced over at Bron to see that he was awake and watching her. He didn't move or blink, but eventually he closed his eyes again, so Ylva waited a few minutes then put one hand on the shape beneath the blanket.

'I'll avenge you,' she whispered. 'I promise.'

Ylva sat dry-eyed and motionless, trying to stay awake because she knew the Mares would bring her bad dreams. But after time, her back slumped, her head dropped, and sleep took her.

7

Hard Earth

Cathryn and Bron were not in the hut when she woke.

Ylva was curled on the dirt floor beside Mother's cold dead body. It took a second to remember where she was and what had happened, and then it crashed over her like a flood of icy water. She sat up and grabbed the bow, startling Geri awake. Blankets lay around her, as if someone had tried to make her comfortable. She panicked, getting to her feet and putting her hand to her throat, but her scarf was still fastened tight.

Light leaked in through the shutters, and there were fresh logs over the embers in the fire pit. A faint and regular scraping came from outside.

Ylva went to open the door, cold air stinging her

nostrils. The morning was still half-dark, as if the world was in need of a clean. Leaden clouds hung low, and mist whispered through the trees. On the track, the surface snow had crystallized and become a layer of crusted jewels.

Two horses were tethered beside the hut, one chestnut, one golden. Both had their heads down as they ate grain from a wooden trough. The sound of their satisfied crunching was soothing – it reminded Ylva of cold mornings in the village at home, feeding the animals and preparing the horses.

As she approached, with Geri at her heels as always, the sweet-smelling golden horse looked up with a lazy turn of its head. Its shaggy hide was beautiful, rippling with shades of autumn, its mane and tail like silver. One fetlock was a single white sock. But what caught Ylva's attention was the symbol painted on to its flank; a white circle, with two tails curled inwards at the bottom.

$$\infty$$

The chestnut horse was painted with the same symbol.

Sometimes the villagers at home used the design on their animals, or wore a similar-shaped charm on a necklace to ward off dangerous magic. Whoever Cathryn was, wherever she came from, she didn't just know about Ylva's gods – she also used familiar symbols.

'You're beautiful.' Ylva ran the flat of her palm down the animal's muscular neck. Soothed by the creature's calm nature, she wanted to stay longer, but the faint and regular scraping she'd heard before continued, so she went to investigate. Her boots crunched the frozen crust of snow as she headed behind the hut where there was a patch of clear land before the trees grew thick and wild up the mountain slope.

Cathryn and Bron were there, both of them with shovels in their hands, digging in the black soil.

When they noticed Ylva, they stopped.

Cathryn jabbed the tip of the shovel into the ground and leant on the handle. 'We put the man in the ground already. Deep, so the animals won't find him.' She looked at the other grave. 'This one is for your mother and—'

'I should do it.' Ylva considered the pile of dark soil. 'It's my duty.'

'Huh,' Cathryn said. 'Maybe you're right.' She pulled the tip of the shovel from the dirt and held it out. 'You can finish while we get breakfast.'

Ylva came forward to take the shovel, but didn't start digging until Cathryn and Bron had left.

Geri sat in silence beside the grave while Ylva dug the hard earth. He stared up at the mountain and didn't make a sound, but it was comforting to know he was there. No one understood Ylva the way Geri did.

When the grave was deep enough, Ylva climbed out and brushed the dirt from her breeches.

'There's warm ale,' Cathryn said as Ylva went back inside the hut. 'And hot stew.' She was standing by the fire, stirring the blackened pot. Bron was sitting at the table, shovelling stew into his mouth with a wooden spoon.

'You're sweating from all that digging,' Cathryn said. 'Why don't you take off your scarf?'

Ylva put a hand to her neck and bunched the wool in her fist. 'No.'

'Suit yourself.' Cathryn ladled steaming stew into a clay bowl and placed it on a flat wooden plate along with a large chunk of cheese. She tore hard bread from a broken loaf to put beside it and held the meal out for Ylva. 'The bread is stale but there's enough there for two people. It'll fill you up.'

When Ylva didn't take it, Cathryn sighed and her face fell into a sad expression. 'Child, I know there are things you want to do, but there's nothing to be gained by doing them on an empty stomach. Sooner or later, everyone must eat.' She extended the plate again. 'Please.'

Mother would have said the same thing but in a different way. If Ylva was going to head into the wilderness on the trail of the three-fingered man, it made sense to do it on a stomach full of hot food. And a meal like this didn't come along every day.

'Survival always comes first, isn't that what your mother told you?' It was as if Cathryn had read her mind. 'Eat now, and then we'll see she gets a proper burial. You have my word on that.'

When Ylva still didn't come forward, Cathryn sighed and put the plate on the edge of the table. She filled her own bowl and sat down to eat.

'You slept hard,' she said between mouthfuls. 'You

were shivering like a wet dog but Bron put blankets over you to keep you warm.'

The boy scowled and concentrated on his food.

'The stew is good,' Cathryn said. 'If you don't take it, I think Bron will eat what I put out for you. He's as skinny as a sapling but he eats like a wolf in winter.'

Despite everything, Ylva's stomach grumbled and the smell of the food made her mouth water. She wanted to not need anything from anyone, for it to be just her and Geri against the world, but the stew smelt a lot better than the soup did last night, and she was sure it wasn't just because she was hungry – it was because Cathryn was a much better cook than the owner of the hut had been.

Take it. Geri nudged against her leg. *You need to be strong.*

Ylva's stomach rumbled again and she finally caved in. She pulled the plate towards her before snatching it up and taking it to the other table.

She wanted the food to be tasteless. The bottom had fallen out of her world, and it was wrong that anything should not be affected by the horror of what had happened. But the food was delicious, and that made her feel small and unimportant, and even more determined to retain Mother's memory.

The world might forget, but she never would.

8

No Tears

After eating, Ylva went to the pile of blankets and spread one flat on the floor.

'Let us help you with that.' Cathryn pulled Bron to his feet.

'No, I don't want—'

'You can't move her on your own,' Cathryn said.

Ylva glared at her, angry because she was right. 'Fine.'

Every time either Cathryn or Bron touched Mother, Ylva's skin crawled as if she were covered in insects, but she allowed them to help lift her body on to the blanket and wrap it around her.

They carried the bundle out to the back of the hut and lowered it into the ground.

Ylva took the bone-handled knife she had found and placed it on Mother's chest. It would protect her in the life that came next.

'Do you want to say some words?' Cathryn asked.

Ylva shook her head and began to shovel the black soil into the grave. The dirt was rich and dark and damp. It dropped on to the blanket with the sound of heavy rain.

Geri stood at the end of the hole, looking in, and when Mother was gone Ylva fell to her knees beside him. 'No tears. This isn't the time.' She put her arms around her best friend and hugged him to her. 'Don't let me cry. I have to be strong. Mother is with the gods now, and I'll see her again one day.'

Cathryn came to stand behind her and reached out a hand. She hesitated, then touched her fingers to Ylva's shoulder, but Ylva shrugged her away.

Cathryn stepped back, letting her hand fall to her side, and they remained that way, in the cold, for a long while.

>>>———————➔

After time, Ylva pressed her hand to the earth in front of her. 'I promise I'll come for you.' She stood and turned to Cathryn. 'Thank you for your help.'

'What do you plan to do now?' Cathryn followed her back into the hut. 'Where will you go?'

Ylva picked up the bow and the quiver of iron-tipped arrows.

'You're not thinking of going out there alone, child,' Cathryn said. 'You can't. Not with revenge in your heart.'

Ylva looked up at her.

'You are, aren't you? I can see it in your eyes.' Cathryn swept a hand towards the dark stain on the floorboards.

'You're going after the people who did this.'

'It's my duty. It's what the gods expect of me; my destiny.'

'You think this is destiny? That the Norns pulled strings to make this happen to you?' Cathryn shook her head. 'What happened here wasn't any kind of destiny; it was murder, and no one expects you to avenge it. Not even your gods.'

'A murder must always be avenged,' Ylva said. 'It's how it is.'

'So you kill him, then one of his people kills you? Is that how it is? And who will avenge your death?'

'What else am I going to do?' Ylva collected her satchel and put it over her shoulder. By the firepit, she crouched to take a pinch of black ash from the edge of the fire. She put it in the palm of her left hand and spat on to it, using a finger to stir it into a dark paste that she spread around each eye. It would help to soften the hard glare of the snow, but it would also make her look fierce, like a Viking.

'Don't be so stupid, child, it's your duty to live, not to die. Do you have any idea how far we are from anything?' Cathryn said.

'I'm not stupid.' Ylva made more of the paste and drew lines running downwards from both corners of each eye, as if she were crying black tears.

'This hut is the warmest place within two days' ride. The nearest you'll find is the settlement at Dunholm. There's not even so much as a farmstead in this wilderness.' Cathryn blocked the door. 'I can't let you walk out into that.'

'You can't stop me.' Ylva tucked the bedroll under her arm and clicked her tongue at Geri. The dog came to her heel but looked up at Cathryn with doleful eyes.

Ylva knew he wanted to stay – *Help us. Protect us* – and a small part of her wanted that too, but she had a job to do. She had a duty.

'No,' she said to him. 'They can't tell me what to do. How can they stop me? Are they going to kill me? Are they going to kill me the way those people killed Mother and—?'

Cathryn reached out but stopped short of touching her. 'Who are you talking to, child? Of course we won't hurt you.'

'Then get out of my way and let me go. I can't stay here, so I have to go out there. I have to do something. I have to go somewhere.'

'Then come with me,' Cathryn said. 'Come with us.' She gestured towards Bron. 'We'll take care of you. If you go out there, you'll get yourself killed. Think about what your mother said; survival always comes first. There's a safe place we can take you that—'

'She also told me it's better to be fearless than faint of heart.'

Cathryn's expression softened. 'But not better to be dead.'

'I have to avenge her.' Ylva's throat was tight. 'It's the way we do things. It's expected. And it's all I have left, so if I die, then I die, and I don't care. You can put me in a saga and tell people how stupid I was.'

'I never understood why you Danes love fighting and fame so much. Why don't you let us take you somewhere safe? We have a place where— '

Bron nudged Cathryn and glared at her. He made the gesture he had used before – his hand by his waist, turning it as if he were throwing something away – and Ylva knew what it meant. It was his hand-speak, his way of saying 'no'. But it felt to Ylva as if it meant so much more.

Get rid of her. Let her go. Let her die.

Well, that was just fine by her. 'I don't need you. I don't need anyone to take care of me.' Ylva stood in front of Cathryn and made herself as tall as she could.

Bron continued to make signs with his hands, Cathryn's expression growing darker as she watched him. When he had finished, Cathryn replied using hand-speak, then looked down at Ylva. 'Please let us help you. Please don't go out there looking for revenge. You have a serpent by the tail, child, and nothing good ever comes from it. Everyone thinks revenge will solve something, make them feel better, and everyone finds out it doesn't. You'll lose everything.'

'I haven't got anything to lose.'

'What about your life?' Cathryn put a hand on Ylva's shoulder. 'You could lose your life. What could be more important than that?'

'I don't like to be touched.' Ylva shrugged the hand away as if it burnt. 'And people die every day, so if the gods want me to die, then that's what'll happen, and there's nothing anyone can do about it. Anyway, I'll be happy to see Mother again.'

'Happy? You don't mean that.' Cathryn resisted when Ylva tried to push past, but Bron went to her and put a hand on the woman's arm.

'Let her go,' he said.

They were the first words he had spoken since arriving at the hut. His voice was soft and hoarse, almost a whisper, and the effort to make the words was clear in his eyes.

Cathryn didn't try again to stop Ylva from leaving. Instead, she followed her into the cold to see her take the first steps on a journey that would lead her closer to hardship and heartache than any child should ever come.

Cathryn watched Ylva walk along the track until she was gone.

Trust

9

Thor's Salvation

Ylva's face burnt with cold, and she hardly saw the land around her as she struggled through the snow. Before long, deep thunder shook the sky and the ashen clouds darkened. Banks of them rolled across the world, smothering it and bringing fresh snow. It fell lightly at first but soon became heavy with flakes that fluttered in the still air. Ylva stopped in the eerie silence and looked up. 'England isn't so different from home,' she said to Geri. 'The people sound different, but the sky is just as grey.' Snow settled on her face and in her hair. As it melted, her skin grew numb and began to sting, so she wiped the moisture away with her sleeve. 'And we have the same trees.'

To the left of the track, rowan and alder grew among the pines that sprouted from the white ground like old, dead limbs. Ylva knew the trees and their names because she had made it her business to know them. Mother had helped her with that. She had understood Ylva's need to know; understood that once she had set her mind on something, it was not easy to encourage her to change it.

To her right, the mountain rose gently, the forest rising with it until the trees gave up trying to grow in the thin soil and left it for the grassy scrub to claim. Higher still, and it was just bare and jagged rock, like a jaw of vicious black teeth biting into the stony sky.

No one had ever been more alone.

Even Geri – faithful Geri – had followed her like a reluctant ghost. Usually he was so brave and full of energy, but instead of foraging ahead, breaking away to investigate the smells of the forest, he had hung back, looking behind them every few minutes. Now he did it again, whining through his nose.

'I know you want to go back,' Ylva told him. 'But we can't. No one else cares, so it's up to me to find the three-fingered man.' Her breath came in clouds that billowed around her face. 'It's like when Thorir Erikson killed Sweyn Witch-Breaker's brother. You remember? Sweyn went straight to Thorir's home, called him outside and cut him down with his axe. It's our way.'

Geri whined again and looked up at Ylva.

It won't bring Mother back, Ylva imagined him saying. *Maybe Cathryn was right. Maybe we should have gone with her. She could have taken us somewhere safe.*

A howl echoed out from the wilderness. A single, sorrowful tune. Ylva turned on the spot, listening for the sound to come again. Geri held his breath and swivelled his ears, but the land remained silent.

Wolves.

'It's a long way off.' Ylva scanned the mountain as snow flurried around her. 'There's nothing to worry about.'

And the wind is getting stronger.

'So I'll move into the edge of the forest where the trees will protect me from the worst of it.' And she would be almost invisible to anyone passing by – if anyone else was mad enough to be travelling this road in such weather.

Wolves are another matter. There's no hiding from wolves.

'Hush.' She moved off the track and continued walking.

⟫⟫⟫⟶

Ylva was half-right about the trees protecting her. The alders and birches sheltered her from the wind, but in the forest, the ground was uneven and dangerous. Twists of root and fists of rock lay beneath the snow like traps.

Ylva fought her fear. She pushed away her sadness and anger, and whispered under her breath, telling herself to be strong and fearless; to be ready for the moment when she would find the three-fingered man.

'Wanderers will tell our story,' she spoke quietly to Geri as she pressed on. 'Just think; jarls and warriors will sit by the fire and listen to the saga of Ylva the Fearless – the girl who hunted and killed the monster that murdered her mother.'

Geri didn't look impressed.

'I'll be remembered for ever,' Ylva said. 'For hundreds

of years.'

I'd rather be warm and safe.

Ylva fell silent, thinking about the hut; about the fire and the warm ale and the breakfast she'd had. She thought about Cathryn and the boy – Bron – and wondered if she had made a mistake. Perhaps she *was* stupid, as Cathryn had said. Perhaps she should have stayed where she was. Perhaps she should have thought more carefully about setting off into the wilderness alone.

Stupid. The word stung. Just thinking about it made her chew the inside of her cheek until it hurt.

Ylva brushed the snow from her shoulders and looked back at her footprints, already disappearing beneath the constant fall of fresh flakes. She shivered and pulled her cloak tighter to stop her body heat from escaping.

Geri whined. *Should we go back?*

'No. Be strong, be fearless, and survive. There's no point in feeling sorry for myself; that's not our way. A true Viking accepts hardship with open arms and laughs in its face.'

I don't feel like laughing.

Ylva didn't feel like laughing, either. She was cold and tired and now she was beginning to wonder if she should return to the hut. If she stayed out here she might freeze to death, and then her saga would be a very short one.

'No.' She pushed the thought away. 'I'm not going back. Come on, Geri, I have an idea. There are other ways for me to keep warm.' She went to the base of a rowan tree, and dropped to her hands and knees. Above her, the dark limbs reached out, laden with blood-red berries.

'Thor's Salvation,' Ylva said. 'That's what Mother called rowan trees, remember? Thor's Salvation.' She dug into the snow, burrowing down to the forest floor, searching for fallen leaves and pine needles, just how Mother had taught her. And as she searched and gathered, she continued to mumble under her breath.

'Don't you remember the story Mother told us about Thor killing the giant Geirrod?' There had been nothing better than listening to Mother's voice as she spun her tales of Thor's strength and Loki's cunning. Ylva would sit on the floor of the longhouse, endlessly grinding corn with the quern while Mother worked the loom and told her of the death of Balder, or how Odin lost his eye.

'There's a part when Thor's carrying Loki across the river Vimur,' Ylva said as she collected leaves into a pile. 'He uses a rowan tree to drag himself out of the river before he goes to find the giant.' She looked at Geri standing beside her. 'So maybe Thor's looking over us now. He'll keep us safe.'

Geri wasn't quite so convinced; he whined and looked back the way they had come, but Ylva wouldn't be discouraged, so she returned to her task, and when she was ready, she stuffed handfuls of the debris between the layers of her breeches, packing it right down to her boots. 'This'll keep me warm.'

Even through the linen, it scratched and prickled like cat's claws, but it would provide extra insulation. Ylva had done this before and she had learnt that, with time, she could grow accustomed to almost anything.

Next, she tightened her belt and stuffed handfuls of leaves between her undershirt and her tunic. Then she unravelled the blanket roll and wrapped it around her body, securing it with twine she had taken from the hut. By the time she hugged her rabbit-fur cloak around her once more, she was already feeling the benefit of the extra layers. But now the day was an hour shorter, and her stomach was starting to complain. Cathryn's stew had kept her going this long, but the cold had drained her energy. She allowed herself a small ration of salted fish from her satchel and a sip from her water bag before setting off once more.

10

Smoke on the Mountain

———➤

Ylva walked. And walked.

From time to time, she paused to nibble at the rations from her satchel, and in those moments, she watched the path and the forest, searching for any sign of passing travellers, but saw nothing.

The animals were quiet. She didn't hear the wolf again. She saw no rabbit tracks, no evidence of deer or fox or boar, and even the birds were silent. The only animal she saw that morning was a magpie that hopped from branch to branch ahead of her before taking to the air and flying away.

When Geri began to complain again, whimpering and stealing glances over his shoulder, Ylva ignored him and occupied herself by counting trees; a game she used to play with Mother.

'What tree is that?' she said to Geri, but he refused to play along. Instead of walking at her heel, he fell behind, moving slowly with his head down and his ears flat.

'Juniper,' she answered for him. 'So that's twelve I've counted now. As well as twenty-two willows, six hazels, and more aspens and birches than I can remember.'

Who cares?

'It gives us something to think about.'

We have something to think about; the hut where it was warm and there was hot food and we wouldn't be alone.

'Well we're not going back, so you can forget about that.'

Geri stopped and looked up at Ylva. *Maybe I'll go back on my own.*

'On your own?' Ylva came to a halt and stared down at her footprints leading away into the past. 'You can't leave me.'

Geri stood tall and glared at her, then turned away from Ylva and started walking in the opposite direction. He followed Ylva's tracks but only managed a short distance before he stopped as if he'd met an invisible wall.

'You can't, can you?' Ylva said.

No. Geri lowered his head.

'And you know why, don't you?'

Yes. Because you need me.

>>>———→

By noon, the storm had finally blown over, and the snow had stopped. The sky remained lifeless and ugly, but the worst of it was gone – for now, at least. Ylva pressed on, watching the faint sun inch lower and lower until it dropped behind the trees and she knew she would have to find a place to make camp.

But as she rounded a bend in the track, she spotted a thin tongue of smoke rising between the trees on a shelf further up the mountain. Ylva dropped to a crouch and watched the grey wisps snaking into the cold air.

'Where there's smoke, there's fire,' Ylva said.

And people.

The only people Ylva had seen in the past two days, apart from Cathryn and the boy, were the people who had killed Mother, so as she stared at the smoke, she imagined the three-fingered man sitting by the fire with the woman. The woman would be wearing Mother's necklace, and the three-fingered man would be holding her knife. In Ylva's mind, they were laughing, and it was her duty to put an end to that.

'We need to get closer.' She broke into a slow run, heading across the track and into the trees on the other side. As soon as she was under cover, she removed the blanket and rolled it into a bundle. She tugged her tunic from her belt, pulled down her outer breeches and shook out all the leaves and pine needles. Whatever happened now, she had to be fast and silent. Like a wolf hunting its prey.

—————→

The slope was gentle, so the climb was easy at first. As she moved higher though, the ground became treacherous, and Ylva grasped at trees to pull herself up the mountainside. Rough bark scratched her already-callused hands. Sharp twigs snagged at her fur cloak.

The air was colder the higher she climbed, and Ylva's

breath came in heavy gulps, but she pushed up and up. This would be in her saga, of course. The difficult climb up the mountainside to confront the three-fingered man. The travelling storytellers would tell it as a long and dangerous journey in a foreign land, lowering their voices to make the listeners draw close around the fire in the great hall.

'Without hesitation, Ylva the Fearless climbed the crooked mountain using the rowan trees for grip, just as Thor used one to cross the Vimur . . .' they would say.

By the time she reached level ground, the sun had dipped below the treetops and the light in the forest was dim and grainy.

Ylva dropped the blanket roll at the base of a papery-barked silver birch, and shrugged off her satchel. She camouflaged her belongings with armfuls of sticks, and put her mouth close to Geri's soft ear.

'We have to be quiet now,' she whispered.

Geri licked his lips and whined.

'Please.' She put her arms around him. 'Not a sound.'

She held him close for a moment, feeling the softness of his fur and breathing his reassuring smell. In that instant she was transported home to a summer's day in her village by the sea, with Mother humming songs as she worked on the loom.

'No.' Ylva released him and put an arrow to the string of her bow. 'I haven't time for that.' She set off towards the smoke.

➤➤➤————➤

Ylva crept through forest understorey thick with shrubs and dogwood. All around, the trees whispered as the wind teased through their knotted branches. The smell of pine and smoke hung in the freezing air.

Ylva felt nothing but the rapid beat of her own heart. She heard nothing but—

'. . . if you ask me . . .'

The snatch of conversation made her stop. She listened hard, but the wind only allowed her those four words. Now there was just the white noise of the forest and the crackle of twigs dropping through the branches. Ylva waited before creeping on into the dying day, and when she was closer to the source of the smoke, she took cover in the low branches of a juniper. Geri pressed in tight between her and the rough-barked trunk.

Through the trees, Ylva saw a small glade, in which two figures sat with their backs to her. The glow of fire washed around them. They were not the ones who had murdered Mother, though. They were both men, and neither of them was big enough to be the three-fingered man.

Ylva had to make a decision: watch a little longer to see if the people were joined by the ones she was looking for, or find somewhere suitable to make camp. The longer she waited, the less light she would have. As it was, there was barely enough time for her to—

Shhhhhhk.

It was the unmistakeable sound of a blade sliding from its sheath.

'You spying on us?'

Ylva let out her breath and lowered her eyes to the ground.

'Take the arrow away from the string, and turn

around. Do it slowly. I'm the nervous type and you don't want to make me jumpy.'

Ylva stayed as she was.

'There's no use pretending I can't see you, or that you didn't hear me. I see you as clearly as I know my own name. That tree isn't going to swallow you up, no matter how close you get to it, so I won't ask again. Do you want to remain in this world, or shall I send you to another?'

Ylva shifted her eyes to see Geri, his black and grey fur camouflaged by the grainy light and the thick foliage of the juniper. 'Stay calm,' she whispered to him. 'Please. And keep quiet. I don't need you right now. I have to be strong.'

'Who are you talking to? Who else is in there?'

'No one.' Ylva stood and turned to face the man. 'There's no one there.'

'Hm.' The man had a hungry look. He was tall and thin, with a narrow face. What little hair was on his dirty head stood up on end as if he'd been struck by lightning. Khol-ringed pale eyes stared from beneath heavy eyebrows. A thick wolfskin cloak was fastened around his shoulders, and he wore sheepskin breeches that made him look like he was half goat. In his right hand, he carried an axe with a bloodstained handle, while his left held a sword pointed towards Ylva.

'You sure there's no one else in there?' Keeping his sword steady, the man edged forward and reached out with his axe to part the branches of the juniper where Ylva had been hiding. He took his eyes off Ylva for no longer than a heartbeat at a time as he searched. 'You were talking to someone.'

'Myself,' Ylva said. 'I talk to myself sometimes.'

'Hm.' Finding nothing, the man stepped back and scanned left and right before finally settling his full gaze on Ylva. He grinned, displaying a set of pointed teeth. 'Are you lost?' He cast his eyes around without moving his head.

'I'm looking for someone,' Ylva said.

'Good. Good. And well done, because you've succeeded – you have found someone.' He made a curious giggling sound and his eyes settled on the bow Ylva was holding. 'But did you find the right someone?'

'Not yet.'

'And you're a Dane.' He kept the sword pointed towards her. 'You don't speak like a Saxon, and you certainly don't look like one.'

'Yes. I am.'

'Well . . .' He glanced over Ylva's shoulder and giggled again. 'The night is getting cold, but we have a good fire, and we have warm ale.' He nodded at the weapon in her hands. 'If you let me take that, you can join us and share.'

'I don't want to join you.' Ylva made a move to step around him, but the man put out his sword and pressed the flat of the blade against her arm to stop her.

He lowered his voice and looked right into her eyes. 'I insist.'

'Arvid, put your sword away.' A voice came from behind. 'You're scaring the poor child.'

One of the men must have left the fire, drawn by the sound of voices, but Ylva didn't take her eyes off the goat-man, and he didn't take his eyes off her. He kept the sword firm against her arm and bared his sharp teeth.

'I told you to put it away,' the second man said as he came to stand beside them. He was taller than the goat-man, broad and strong, with a kind face. He stared at Arvid the goat-man and put his hand on the blade of the sword until Arvid finally lowered it and slipped it back into its sheath.

Shhhhhhk.

'Good. Can't you see she's just a child?' The second man ran a hand down his thick dark beard and smiled at Ylva. His teeth were not filed to points like the goat-man's, but they were marked by thick horizontal grooves with red dye etched into them. 'We don't want to hurt you,' he said.

'Then you'll let me go on my way.' Ylva kept the arrow against the string of her bow.

'We won't stop you.' The man opened his hands and clapped them together. 'But it's getting darker with every breath we take, and it's colder than Niflheim.' He rubbed his palms hard as if to warm them. 'I can see you shivering, and I feel it deep in my own bones.' He looked around. 'And there are wolves in these forests. It's no place for a man to be alone, never mind a child.'

'I can take care of myself.'

'I don't doubt it – you're a Dane – but why give yourself the trouble? Why put yourself in danger?' The man thought for a moment. 'Here's what I suggest; you're a warrior, I can see that, so we'll let you keep your weapons. Hold an arrow against your bowstring for as long as you like, and keep the axe in your belt so you're prepared for whatever may come, but join us at the fire, sit for a while, eat some of our kill, drink some warm ale, and then . . .' He shrugged. 'Then go on your way if that's what you want to do. We won't stop you.'

Ylva searched his eyes for the lie then glanced over his shoulder at the glow of the fire. Her body was infected with cold. It ran through her veins. Everything was numb and exhausted. The fire called out to her, and now there was a smell of cooked meat drifting in the air, making her stomach rumble. Maybe she should go to the fire and talk to these men.

'All right,' she said. 'But I know how to use this, and I'll shoot you sooner than I'd shoot a rat.'

The man smiled. 'I'll lead the way.'

11

Three Brothers

The third man was roasting rabbits on skewers over the fire at the far edge of the glade. Barrel-chested, round-stomached, and wide-faced, he had a moustache to be proud of.

'My brother Varg,' said the man with the kind face. 'We call him Varg the Stout, and I'm sure you can see why. You already met my brother Arvid.' He waved a hand at the half-goat man. 'And you can call me Halvor.' He sat down on a fallen tree and held his hands out towards the fire. 'Sit. Get yourself warm.'

As the three men took their places, Ylva glanced around their camp. Their sheepskin bedrolls were in an arc on the other side of the fire, and three shields rested against the far end of the tree trunk, their decorated faces turned away from her. There were helmets, spears, and a couple of satchels. A trio of mangy horses was hobbled close by.

Outside the camp, away from the fire, a young black-haired man knelt at the base of a tree. He wore a pair of dirty breeches and a torn shirt, but nothing else. He looked like a Saxon, and Ylva thought he was praying to his Christian god, until she realized he was tied. His wrists and ankles were bound behind him, forcing him into a permanent hunch, and he was unable to control his shivering.

When Ylva didn't sit, Varg the Stout invited her once more. 'You can relax,' he said. 'We won't hurt you. Drink. Eat.' He held out a cup of ale in one hand and a cooked rabbit leg in the other.

Ylva's mouth watered and she could almost taste the roasted meat, but she stayed where she was.

'Well, all right,' Varg the Stout said. 'Sit, stand, hop on one foot, it makes no difference to us. Skol.' He raised the cup to his lips and drained it.

Arvid, the goat-man with the pointed teeth, leant over and squirted a big gob of spit at one of the hot rocks that ringed the fire. He wiped his mouth with his sleeve and watched it hiss and bubble.

Once more, Ylva glanced over at the man tied at the base of the tree. 'Who is he?' she asked.

Halvor took a skewered rabbit from the fire and bit into it. 'He's a murderer.' He wiped grease from his beard with the back of his hand.

'A murderer?' Ylva studied the wretched man. 'Who did he murder?'

'What does it matter?' He raised his voice so the

wretched man could hear him. 'We've followed him more than five days across Midgard, and now we have him.'

'So, you're hunters?' Ylva came closer and perched on a rock opposite the three men. She put the bow across her lap and held her hands towards the fire. 'Hunters of men?'

'You could say that.' Halvor's eyes shone in the glow of the fire.

'Then maybe you can help me.'

'Help you?' Halvor took another bite. 'How might we do that?'

'I'm looking for someone. Two people, in fact. A man and a woman. They're also murderers who need to be brought to justice – they killed my mother. Men like you could help me find them.'

'Why would we do that?' Arvid grinned, letting Ylva see his pointed teeth. 'What's in it for us?'

On the other side of the small glade, the forest was in shadow. The sun was finally gone from the day and Ylva could see no more than a few paces into the trees. She was huddled in a small cocoon of light in a dark, cold world, and as she watched the shadows, Geri crept into view, head down, and stopped just outside the circle.

Don't trust them.

'Well?' Arvid asked again. 'What's in it for us?'

Don't trust them.

Ylva ignored the voice in her head. 'Silver,' she said.

The three men sat up a little straighter.

'Silver?' Halvor swallowed and held the skewered rabbit poised in front of his mouth. 'You have silver with you? How much?'

'I'm not stupid; I don't have it with me. My father has it in Dunholm. He's a jarl. As brave as a berserker, and as strong as ten men.'

'A jarl in Dunholm?' Halvor said.

'Yes.' Ylva picked at the skin around her fingernail. 'That's where we were headed when those people I told you about killed Mother. My father will pay you.'

'You're a long way from Dunholm,' Arvid said.

'Wait,' Halvor stopped him. 'Let me make sure I understand.' He lowered the rabbit and stroked his beard. 'You're saying that if we help you find the people who killed your mother, you'll pay us. Once we get to Dunholm, that is, where your strong, brave father will be waiting for us with his hands full of silver.'

'Yes.' Ylva glanced across at Geri standing in the shadows.

'She thinks we're idiots.' Varg the Stout tore a leg off his own rabbit. 'There's no jarl in Dunholm. Her father's probably some useless farmer who couldn't even lift an axe.' He put the whole thing into his mouth, sucked off the meat, and threw the bones over his shoulder.

'He is a jarl,' Ylva said. 'He's Thorin Andersen. Thorin the Fearless. He's brave and strong, and made his riches raiding Christian abbeys and killing Saxons.'

'And I suppose he has a great army of Vikings,' said Varg the Stout.

'Exactly.'

'Even bigger than the Great Army.'

'No,' Ylva said. 'Not that big, but—'

'Dunholm is a Saxon town, there's no jarl there.'

Arvid snorted and spat again.

'He's not in Dunholm,' Ylva said. 'He's near Dunholm. He's going to attack it.'

Arvid laughed at that. 'Well, wherever he is, if this Thorin the Fearless was so rich and strong, we'd have heard of him. And why would he pay us to help you, when he has an army of warriors to send after these murderers?'

'I want to make him proud of me,' Ylva said. 'It's what the gods expect of me.'

'The gods,' Arvid scoffed. 'What do you know about the gods? And if you're a jarl's daughter, then I'm Balder the Beautiful.'

'Wait.' Halvor stopped him again. 'Let's say for the sake of argument that you really do have a rich father in Dunholm, and that we agree to help you.' He looked at his brothers. 'How exactly will we know when we find the people who killed your mother?'

'I'll recognize them.'

'But what if we found these people and you weren't there for some reason? How would we know them? So we could catch them for you, you understand.'

Ylva held up her hand and hesitated. Once again, she looked across at Geri standing on the edge of the circle of light.

Don't trust them.

'You see something?' Varg the Stout glanced over his shoulder and scanned the trees before turning back to Ylva. 'You keep looking back there. What are you looking at?'

'Nothing.'

'You sure she was alone?' Varg asked his brother.

'I'm sure of it,' Arvid told him.

'You searched properly?'

'Of course. You think I'm an idiot?'

Halvor hushed them and spoke to Ylva. 'You were going to tell us what they look like. The people who killed your mother.'

'Yes.' Ylva ignored Geri and slowly folded down her two smallest fingers. 'The man only has three fingers on his right hand.'

'A three-fingered man?'

'Yes. And both he and the woman wore scarves over their mouths, with half-skulls painted on them. Wolf skulls.'

'Wolf skulls?' Halvor put down his food and leant forwards.

'Exactly,' Ylva said.

Halvor frowned. 'And you're sure this man and this woman murdered your mother?'

By the trees, Geri curled back his lips to show his teeth. His ears flattened against his head, and the fur on his back bristled.

'Do you know them?' Ylva asked.

'Yes we do.' Halvor put his greasy fingers into his collar and pulled up his scarf. 'They're friends of ours.'

12

Be Careful
Who You Trust

Ylva stared at the half-skull design on Halvor's scarf while thoughts tumbled in her head like snowflakes in a storm. She had been stupid, just as Cathryn said. She had come into the wilderness alone, and she had trusted when she shouldn't have trusted. Geri's instincts were right. These Vikings were friends with the three-fingered man, the person who had murdered Mother, and now they would kill her.

As soon as that thought was clear in her head, her hand was moving. Ylva raised the bow from her lap, drawing the string as quickly as she could. She turned it towards the three men, releasing the arrow before it was level.

Fired in haste, the iron-tipped arrow went wide of its target . . . but only just. It clipped Arvid's neck with enough impact and surprise to knock him backwards from his perch on the fallen tree.

With the pinch of the string still humming on her fingers, Ylva jumped to her feet and reached for the quiver on her back. She fumbled to pull a second arrow free, but Halvor was too quick. Before she put the arrow to the string, he was across the fire, stepping through the flames to grab the bow and rip it from her hands.

'What are you doing?' he growled through his teeth as he threw it aside.

Ylva didn't stop. She raised the arrow in her fist, thrusting the sharp point at Halvor's eyes.

'No.' Halvor sidestepped and gripped her wrist. He twisted, forcing Ylva to drop the arrow, and pinned her arm to her side. 'Stop.' For a second, it worked. The strength of his hand, the force of his voice, and the hardness of his stare were enough to make her stop.

Ylva looked over at Geri who stood with his head low, his paws spread apart, his legs rigid. His teeth flashed in the firelight, and Ylva wished more than anything that he could help her, but there was nothing he could do. She had to fight alone. So she renewed her struggle against Halvor, moving her free hand up to grab for the knife on her belt.

'No!' he shouted again as he snatched her other arm, almost lifting her off the ground. 'What's the matter with you?'

Behind him, Varg the Stout helped Arvid to his feet. The goat-man's expression hung between surprise and anger as he touched his neck and looked at his fingers, dark with blood. When he glared across the fire at Ylva, though, the anger took over. He pushed Varg away from him and came at her, drawing a large dirty knife from his belt.

He yanked Ylva from Halvor's grip and threw her down into the snow. Dropping his weight on top of her, he put one knee either side to pin her. 'Right now you're thinking you shouldn't have come to sit by our fire,' he hissed. 'Talking about killing our friend.'

'Hold on, Arvid,' Halvor said. 'Just wait. Calm down.' But neither Arvid nor Ylva were listening. Their full focus was on each other. Nothing else mattered.

Ylva struggled and kicked but Arvid kept her pinned to the ground. And as she fought against him, her cloak opened and the scarf loosened from around her neck.

'I knew it,' he sneered when he saw what Ylva was hiding. 'You're exactly what I thought you were. Now stop squirming like an eel and let me tell you something I've learnt about killing.' Arvid put the knife against Ylva's throat, just above her collar, and bared his teeth at her like a wild animal.

She stopped.

'It's much more satisfying when you're up close like we are now. Looking right into someone's eyes when they get snuffed out like a—' Arvid blew stale breath in Ylva's face. He frowned, puzzled, and all his meanness disappeared in an instant. The knife fell from his hand.

'Arvid?' Halvor asked. 'What's the matter with you?'

Arvid's eyes widened and he looked down at his chest.

Released from his hypnotic stare, Ylva followed his gaze and saw the blackened iron arrowhead protruding from his furs. It took a second for her to understand what she was seeing, and in that short time, Varg the Stout stiffened beside her and took a quick breath just as Arvid had done. Ylva snapped her head round to see that he too had an arrowhead sticking through the front of his cloak.

Halvor didn't waste time worrying about his Viking brothers; he spun on the spot, drawing his sword. 'Come out where I can see you! Come out here and—'

A third arrow hummed across the clearing and slammed into him. Halvor grunted and staggered backwards, but remained standing. He steadied himself and raised his sword. Fury was raging in his eyes as he opened his mouth and let out a terrifying battle cry. But the sound was cut short when the fourth arrow struck him in the heart. His hands dropped to his sides, the sword slipped from his grip, and he fell to his knees in the snow. He wavered for a moment then collapsed forward on to his face.

Ylva secured her scarf, struggled out from beneath Arvid's body, and pushed up on her elbows to see Geri sitting calmly at the edge of the forest on the other side of the glade. As she watched, a lean figure appeared, spirit-like, from the trees and slipped past Geri without pausing. Driven by her instinct to survive, Ylva turned on to her front and scrambled to where her own bow had landed when Halvor threw it away. She ran her hands through the snow until she grasped hold of it. With cold fingers, she pulled an arrow from the quiver and put it to the string as she turned around, drawing the bow ready to shoot at the figure that was now running across the glade towards her.

And when he came into the light cast by the fire, Ylva saw him clearly.

Bron.

The boy moved around the fire without making a sound. He stopped where Halvor lay and nudged him with the toe of his boot, then looked up as Cathryn emerged from the trees and came across the clearing, sword in hand. She went straight to Arvid and Varg, jabbing the tip of her sword into them to make sure they were dead.

'Good job,' Cathryn said to Bron. 'Now go cut that poor boy free.' As she spoke, Geri stood and trotted over to where Ylva lay. He sniffed at her face, nuzzling his nose against her ear, but she kept her arrow pointed at Cathryn.

'I thought they were going to kill me.' Ylva's hands were shaking. 'I didn't know what to do.'

Bron retrieved his arrows and went to the prisoner. He took out his knife, ready to cut him loose, but when he crouched beside the prone figure, he stopped.

'What is it?' Cathryn asked.

Bron looked back and shook his head.

'Dead?'

The boy hugged himself and pretended to shiver.

'The cold?'

Bron nodded.

'Does it ever end?' Cathryn hung her head for a moment. She rubbed her face with one hand then sheathed her sword and turned to Ylva. 'You can stop pointing that thing at me; I'm not going to hurt you. I told you that already.'

Ylva didn't lower the bow – she couldn't. It was as if she were frozen in place. So Cathryn came to her and encouraged her to relax the string. She took the bow from Ylva's hands before grabbing her arm and hauling her to her feet.

'They're dead,' Ylva said. 'All dead.'

'And you're lucky not to be dead too. I warned you not to go off on your own, getting yourself into trouble. Didn't I tell you revenge is a dangerous serpent? That it's likely to turn around and bite you? Look what happened.'

'What does it feel like?' Ylva couldn't turn away. It was as if she had to see.

'Being dead?'

'Killing someone.'

'For you?' Cathryn shook her head. 'I don't know, but maybe it's a good thing you just wounded this one.' She poked Arvid with the toe of her boot. 'Otherwise you'd know for sure.'

Ylva stepped closer to Arvid's body, but Cathryn grabbed the back of her cloak to hold her back. 'We need to get away from here, child. There'll be others around here somewhere and the shouting is sure to have brought them running.'

Ylva tried to pull away. 'Don't touch me.' She glared up at the bear-like woman. 'I don't like to be touched.'

'I'm not touching you, I'm touching your furs, and I'm not letting go because I see what you're thinking.' Cathryn struggled to hold on to her. 'It's the same as you were thinking last time – revenge – but it was a bad idea then and it's a bad idea now. Look around you, child. It's better if you stick with us. There's more out here to be afraid of than just men.'

Wilderness

13

Flames and Screams

'Let go of me.' Ylva fought against Cathryn as she dragged her away from the camp and back into the trees. 'Let go of me! Get off!'

By the time they reached the place where Cathryn and Bron had left their horses, Bron had already removed the hobble from one and was working on the other.

Cathryn finally released her grip, and Ylva tumbled away from her, jamming her hands into her own tangled hair and tugging until it hurt. She squeezed her eyes shut and tipped her head back, opening her mouth wide in a silent scream. Her whole body was tense, every muscle tightening.

'What's the matter with you?' Cathryn asked.

'I told you I don't like to be touched.' Ylva spoke

through gritted teeth. She kept her eyes on Geri and tried not to shout; tried to stay calm. She tightened her hands into fists. 'I don't like it. I can feel you breathing, and smell your stink. Just hearing you swallow your own spit makes me want to—' She crouched and pulled Geri towards her, rocking him gently, searching for his calm comfort.

'You told me not to trust those men,' she whispered to him. 'You told me not to trust them.'

It's all right. Take a deep breath. It's all right.

'I should have listened to you.' She concentrated on his breathing, in and out, the way she did when Thor's chariot was making thunder in the sky, or if the men were drinking and fighting in the village. 'Don't leave me.'

I'm here.

She closed her eyes and took a deep breath of cold forest air, and in that moment she loved Geri with all her heart and she was filled with an overwhelming sadness that ached in every fibre of her body.

When she opened her eyes, she couldn't look at him because she knew it would make her want to cry. And she absolutely refused to allow tears to come to her eyes. This wasn't the time. Instead, she stood and adjusted her scarf. She pushed the hair out of her face, then snatched her bow from Cathryn's hand and stared at the woman as if nothing had happened. 'What do we do now?'

Cathryn narrowed her eyes. 'Are you all right?'

'I'm fine.'

'Doing that makes you feel calm? Talking to yourself?'

'Yes. What do we do now?'

Cathryn eyed her suspiciously. 'Well . . . we need to

get away from here before others arrive. Those warriors were part of a bigger group who won't be happy to find their friends dead in the snow. I'll take you somewhere safe, that's a promise.'

'I don't want to go somewhere safe,' Ylva said. 'I want to find the three-fingered man and avenge Mother.'

'Child, you're making it very difficult for me to like you. You almost died back there. Bron had to kill three men to keep you alive. Three. I don't think you can manage on your own; you need to come with us.'

Bron sighed his disapproval, and swung up on to the chestnut horse, but Cathryn waved a hand at him. 'Hush, you. We won't leave her out here on her own.'

'I won't go with you,' Ylva said. 'If I do, the three-fingered man will get away and I'll never find him. Geri and I will stay here and go after him.'

'Geri?' Cathryn and Bron shared a glance. 'Who's—?'

Bron pointed two fingers at the ground beside Ylva and moved them backwards and forwards.

'The dog?' Cathryn looked at Ylva. 'Geri is the dog?'

Ylva lowered her eyes. 'Yes.'

'I understand . . . I think. But we need to leave now.' Cathryn took her horse's reins and put her foot in the stirrup. With a creak of leather, she hoisted herself up and held out her hand for Ylva. 'You can ride with me. Can your dog keep up?'

Bron made a clicking sound with his tongue to attract Cathryn's attention. He cupped a hand behind his ear before pointing two fingers into the forest behind them.

'You hear something?' Cathryn asked.

Bron turned to the left, then the right, pointing and touching his ears. His eyes were so wide Ylva could see the whites, even in the darkness.

'All sides?' Cathryn steadied the horse and turned to scan the forest.

Bron nodded.

'Quickly.' Cathryn extended her hand to Ylva again. 'Climb up. They've found us.'

Ylva hesitated. She looked at Geri, then up at the wild Saxon woman on her horse. Beside her, Bron was gesturing with his hands again, and Ylva didn't need to understand his hand-speak to know what he was saying. He was telling Cathryn to hurry up. Something bad was about to happen.

As he gestured, a flame appeared in the darkness of the trees close by. One moment it wasn't there, and then it was. A flickering flame, at just the right height for it to be held by a man on horseback. A fraction of a second later, another burst into life nearby.

'Get on, child,' Cathryn said. 'Now.'

More flames appeared – five or six of them – forming a semicircle in the forest behind them, as if angry spirits were materializing.

'Who is it?' Ylva spun around.

'Fairies,' Cathryn said. 'Who do you think? It's people who want to kill us!'

It was enough to make Ylva move. She ignored Cathryn's hand and grabbed the back of the saddle to pull herself up. There was no time for her to settle before Cathryn nudged her horse into a trot.

It was dangerous to ride through the forest at night.

Visibility was low, and there were hazards everywhere. But they had to escape. The horses would see better than their riders – they would have to trust the animals to find a safe route.

As Cathryn and Bron gathered speed, encouraging their horses to move faster, flames flickered in the forest, and the dark shapes of riders blurred beneath them. When Ylva dared to look around, she counted six but it was impossible to be sure. They were moving at such speed it felt as if there were so many more than that; as if a circle of fiery horrors was tightening around them.

Close behind, something let out an ugly scream; a shrill and demonic sound that ripped through Ylva like a blunt-toothed saw. It made her think of draugar rising from their graves to kill anything that crossed their path, and she would swear she even smelt the scent of decay. The sound was followed by a guttural whooping and growling, and when it faded, Ylva's world was filled with nothing but shimmering fire and thundering hooves.

14

Spears of Moonlight

———————➤

Their horses crashed through the understorey. They
thundered between spears of bone-pale moonlight that cut through the canopy, moving from
dark to light and then dark again. The trust between
Cathryn and her horse was strong. She spoke to it in
urgent whispers, squeezing its flanks with her boot
heels, encouraging it to run blindly into the night.

Ylva hated being so close to the woman, it made her
skin itch and tighten as if spiders had burrowed into it,
but she bit her bottom lip and forced herself to dig her
hands deep into Cathryn's furs, hanging on to keep
herself from falling.

Bron had broken ahead of them. As Cathryn's horse
veered sideways, skidding on exposed rocks and tree
roots, Ylva caught a glimpse of the boy disappearing

into the murky gloom. Behind, the terrifying sound began again; a mixture of growling and yipping and screaming. Like hungry wolves fighting over a carcass.

'Be fearless.' She spoke to Geri, who was lost in the darkness behind her. 'Be fearless.' But she knew she was speaking to herself.

Ylva kept her face low behind Cathryn's wide back to shield her from tree limbs that snatched at her like dragon claws as they passed. But when the screaming began again, she risked a look back and immediately regretted it. A talon-like birch branch pulled her hair and tore across her cheek, making her cry out in pain. Her head snapped back, her grip loosened on Cathryn, and Ylva slipped sideways. For one awful, awful moment, she was falling. She was going to plunge into the brambles, and she would be trampled and killed and left for the monsters on their tail.

As she fell, Ylva frantically snatched at Cathryn's cloak, yanking the woman to one side. Startled, Cathryn tugged hard on the reins and the horse responded by swinging left with a suddenness that almost threw both riders from its back. But Cathryn was strong and experienced. Her bond with the animal was firm. She righted herself and reached back to pull Ylva up into the saddle. Immediately, Ylva grabbed a handful of the woman's furs and pressed herself closer for safety.

The damp warmth of her own blood slid down her cheek.

Behind them, the sounds continued. That nightmare of screaming and howling. Some faded into the distance, as if whatever was chasing them had slowed, but others were gaining.

'They're coming closer.' Ylva's voice was full of panic.

And then it was right behind them. A scream that froze her blood. And into that pure white terror came the glint of moonlight on metal as a spear whisked past and thumped into a tree. Bark and woodchips exploded just inches from her face, peppering her with splinters.

'They're catching up!' she shouted as a second spear clattered among the branches to her right.

A rider was moving parallel to them through the trees. He wasn't carrying a flaming torch, but as he pounded in and out of the shafts of moonlight cutting through the birches and aspens, Ylva caught glimpses of him sitting astride his horse, and she saw the terrible image beneath his well-worn helmet. Only the man's eyes were exposed to the cold air of the wintry night; the rest of his face was covered with a black woollen scarf pulled right up over his nose, and it was painted with the same design she had seen outside the hut.

A half-skull.

Ylva screamed at herself to move. This could be him, the three-fingered man, riding alongside her. This might be her chance to fulfil the promise she had made to Mother; to do what the gods expected of her. They had led her to this moment so she could prove herself to them.

Ylva let go of Cathryn and reached for the bow across her back. As she did so, Cathryn drew her sword. The Viking half-skull veered closer, taking advantage of a gap in the trees. He thundered towards them, raising his cruel sword and letting out a savage scream.

In one quick movement, Cathryn slashed her sword at the approaching rider. It was not a good strike. The half-skull saw it before Cathryn had unleashed it, and he slowed his horse at just the right moment. Cathryn's weapon hacked nothing but cold air, and the giant remained firmly on the back of his huge black stallion.

The momentum of her attack unbalanced Cathryn, and as she tried to resettle herself, her horse passed between the narrow white trunks of two aspens growing close together. There was barely enough room for the horse to make it through the gap, but with Cathryn's arm extended, they didn't have a chance.

Still trying to shrug the bow from over her shoulder, Ylva saw what was going to happen. She saw it, but there was nothing she could do to stop it. They were moving too fast, and the trees were too close.

Cathryn's arm smashed into the aspen trunk with a lurching thump followed by a sickening crack. The sword tore from her hand and was lost to the forest. Cathryn screamed and twisted hard in the saddle, forced sideways by the impact. She pushed against Ylva, and the two of them were ripped from the saddle. The horse stumbled, and then they were falling.

15

Two Arrows

Ylva's world was in chaos. She had no sense of where she was or what was happening; whether she was facing forwards or backwards, up or down. A moment of weightlessness stretched to last a lifetime, and the world tumbled. There was the horrible demonic wailing, and Cathryn's screaming, but the overriding sound in her head was the sharp crack she'd heard; the sound of something snapping inside Cathryn's body.

And then bone-crunching impact.

Tangled together, they struck the ground like a fallen beast. Ylva landed hard on her back, the air whooshing out of her lungs, and Cathryn came down on top of her. Before Ylva could take another breath, the two of them were rolling and skidding through the snow. Ice

scattered from shrubs and undergrowth as they barrelled through it and slammed into the thick trunk of a
sturdy oak.

Muddled and dazed, Ylva wondered if the sky had
fallen on her head. But it was Cathryn's bodyweight that
crushed her, and Cathryn's furs that smothered her. Ylva
felt the dreadful closeness of the woman and, in a rising
panic, pushed her away with both hands, twisting and
fighting for breath. It took a huge effort to move her,
and when Ylva was finally free, she sucked in a great
lungful of cold, clean air.

But her problems were not over.

Heart thumping like Thor's hammer, Ylva was lying
upside down against the tree. Her head and back were in
the snow, while her bottom and legs were pressed
against the gnarled trunk. Her muscles were already
tender and bruised where she had fallen. She wriggled
and slipped sideways into the bracken. Thorns snagged
her clothes and pulled her hair. They scratched her
hands and face.

She got to her knees and looked about, scanning the
forest as if she were deep underwater. Her vision was
hazy, her thoughts unclear, but she didn't have time to
waste. Nothing had changed. The warriors were still
hunting them. They still had to make their escape.

Cathryn's horse had deserted them. It was already
thundering riderless into the forest, probably terrified
by what had happened.

'Are you still alive?' Cathryn mumbled.

'I think so.' Ylva looked away from the horse disappearing into the night and stared at the woman who

had come to her rescue. She was like a beast; huge in her furs, with wild hair full of snow and pine needles.

'Good. We need to get moving.' Cathryn grimaced as she tried to stand up. Her right arm was hanging useless by her side. 'This isn't finished. Look.'

In the trees behind them, the monstrous half-skull had turned his horse and was heading straight for them.

Ylva wanted to hide, but there was something burning in her. Something that wouldn't allow her to run away. She was Ylva the Fearless; skalds and wanderers would tell her saga in the great halls of villages all over Midgard. Now was her time for revenge.

She wrestled the bow from over her shoulder. The weapon was still intact, so she knew the gods were with her. And when she reached to take an arrow from the quiver, she was even more sure of it, because although most of the arrows had scattered when she fell, the gods had left her with two.

One more than she needed.

Without thinking, Ylva put an arrow to the bowstring and drew it back. The world moved as if the gods had slowed time. She was about to make history. Ylva the Fearless was about to kill the three-fingered man. The horse and rider thundered towards her, the half-skull lifting his sword ready to strike. Steam bellowed from his horse's nostrils and he shrieked his terrifying battle cry.

Ylva released her arrow.

16

Too Many

Moonlight glinted on the iron tip as it left the bow to flash through the trees. The feathered fletchings fluttered as the arrow spun straight and true.

But the gods weren't with Ylva in that moment. The half-skull's horse stumbled on the ground beneath the snow, skewing to one side, and the arrow zipped past the rider. It ruffled the fur of his cloak as it passed him, but if he noticed, he didn't show it. He rode on, swinging his sword.

Ylva felt the blade carve through the air above her head as she ducked. It bit into the tree beside her, throwing up bark, and then the half-skull was behind her, slowing his horse and turning.

'Get behind the tree!' Cathryn yelled. 'Stay low!'

Ylva reached for the second arrow, but before she could put it to the bow, the rider was on her again, swinging his sword as he passed.

For a second time, Ylva ducked beneath the deadly blade, feeling the weight of it above her and sensing its power as it struck the tree, gouging splinters of wood.

She spun on the spot, twisting and throwing herself behind the tree as the Viking slowed and turned for another attack.

'You sure you know how to use that?' Cathryn looked at the weapon clutched in Ylva's hands.

'I almost hit him,' she said between breaths.

'Almost isn't good enough. Let me take it.'

'With your arm like that?' Ylva flinched as something struck the other side of the tree and the horrible screaming erupted in the forest once more. 'I'll do it myself.'

'Make it count.'

Ylva steeled herself and leant out just enough to peer around the tree, but saw immediately that one arrow wasn't going to be enough; there were two riders out there now. They were close, and moving slowly through the understorey, but both riders wore half-skulls across their mouths. Either one of them could be the three-fingered man. Or perhaps, neither.

Confused, she looked from one to the other, aware that far off to her right, more flames flickered among the trees. Other riders were heading this way, drawn by the terrible sound made by the two half-skulls.

'What are you waiting for?' Cathryn said. 'Shoot him.'

'Which one?' Ylva watched the two men, then

glanced at the approaching flames. The half-skulls were moving closer to one another, coming together and heading towards the tree Ylva and Cathryn were using for protection. The others would be here within a few minutes.

Cathryn struggled to pull an axe from her belt. 'Do it!'

'They're not close enough. I have to kill the right one.' Ylva tucked herself in a crouch against the tree and held the bow so it was pointing upwards – about the height she expected the riders to be at when they appeared.

'What are you doing?' Cathryn said. 'We can't wait for them, there's too many. Fire it off to give us cover and we'll make a run for it.'

As she said it, the head of the first horse came into view around the tree to Ylva's right. Ylva clamped her jaw tight and aimed the bow, ready to shoot. Any moment now the rider would come into view and Ylva would fire. She might not be able to kill both of them, but she would at least kill one. She would—

'Put it down.'

It hadn't occurred to Ylva that the half-skulls would appear on either side of the tree. And it hadn't occurred to her that one would come on foot.

'I won't ask twice. Throw it out into the snow.'

When Ylva turned, she knew she was beaten.

The Viking standing over Cathryn was not big enough to be the three-fingered man, but he was just as terrifying. Dressed in a heavy leather tunic and breeches, he wore a dirty helmet that covered his whole face. The half-skull was painted on it, grinning at Ylva like he was part draugr, part wolf. He held a black shield in one hand, painted with the familiar design, and in the other, he brandished a vicious sword.

'Throw it out,' Cathryn said as she dropped her axe. 'Do what he says.'

Ylva hesitated.

'If you want to get out of this alive, do what he says.'

As far as Ylva was concerned, she lived only for revenge, and if she died now, Mother's murder would not be avenged. This was not her time to die, so she threw the bow aside. As soon as it broke the surface frost, it disappeared beneath the snow and was gone for good.

'We've been looking for you.' The second half-skull appeared, this one still mounted. He also wore a full helmet to cover his face, and carried a short spear.

'Call the others,' said the man on foot.

The rider paused, shifting in the saddle as he watched Cathryn. He nodded and put back his head, letting out a terrible warbling scream that echoed around the forest.

The sound cut deep into Ylva's bones. It shuddered in her teeth and made her heart tremble. But that awful wailing vibration came to an abrupt, burbling stop when something appeared in the rider's neck.

Before Ylva had time to register that it was an arrow, she heard a rush of wind, a thump, and whipped her head around to see that the man on foot had also grown an arrow from his neck. He turned on the spot, dropped his sword into Cathryn's lap, then fell to his knees, grasping at the arrow.

The man on horseback slipped sideways in the saddle until he was resting his head against the tree. His horse stepped forward and the man slipped further, coming out of the saddle and falling. One foot was still caught in the stirrup, and he lay with his leg twisted, his head buried in the snow. When his animal took another disinterested step forward, the rider was dragged alongside it.

Cathryn snatched up the sword that had fallen into her lap. She raised it to point beyond Ylva, but when Ylva turned, she saw the dark-skinned boy creeping from the trees as if he were part of the night. He came crouched and silent, bow held ready. He turned his head from side to side as he scanned the forest.

'Bron.' Cathryn lowered her weapon.

When the boy reached Cathryn's side, he grabbed her sword arm to pull her to her feet.

'Careful,' Cathryn said. 'I think my right arm's broken.'

Bron eased off as he helped her up, but as soon as she was standing, he pointed to the flames flickering through the trees.

'I see them,' Cathryn said. 'We have to go.' She looked around, eyes finally settling on Ylva. 'You know how to ride?'

'Of course. But we should stay here. Fight them.'

'Fight them? You want to fight a horde of battle-hardened warriors?'

'But Bron's already killed . . .' Ylva counted in her head. 'Five. How many more are there?'

'Too many. And the only reason Bron had to kill those men was to save your scrawny bones. Mine too. No, we're not staying here to die.'

'Then you go. I'll wait for them. Give me a—'

'Don't make me angry, child.'

'I'm not a child.'

'Well whatever you are, I never met an animal as stubborn as you. All you have to show for your day is a cut across your cheek, five dead men, and me with a broken arm. And I lost my horse. I'd say that's enough for one day, wouldn't you? Now, I'm not going to stay here, and I'm not going let you stay here either. You have to know when you're beaten, child. Admit it and move on. A good warrior knows when to retreat and live to fight another day.'

Cathryn turned to Bron. 'My horse is gone. You still have yours?'

Bron nodded.

'So this is what we're going to do. Get back on your horse and head north-east for an hour or two before turning north. We'll take these –' she gestured at the animals belonging to the two dead men '– and head north-west.'

Bron made the throwing-away gesture with his right hand by his waist. He did it several times before he pointed at Cathryn, then at himself. After that, his hands moved so quickly Ylva hardly saw the signs he was making.

'No.' Cathryn stopped him. The tightness of her voice betrayed her pain. 'We can't ride together. It's impossible to cover our tracks in this snow.'

Bron's expression darkened and he continued to sign.

'You're wrong.' Cathryn shook her head. 'If we split up, they'll have to split up too. We double our chances. Leave false trails, run circles around them. With luck it'll snow again before morning and cover our tracks. That'll make it even harder for them.' As she spoke, she shoved the sword into her belt, picked up her axe, and trudged over to grab the reins of the horse with the dead man still tangled in the stirrups. She held the horse steady. 'Bron. Get him loose.'

Bron sighed and threw his hands down.

'Now, Bron. We have to go.'

The boy made it clear he disagreed, but came over and freed the body anyway. When that was done, he hurried off to grab the other man's horse. He brought it back to Ylva and held the reins towards her.

Ylva looked at them hanging over his open hand. If she took them, it meant leaving the three-fingered man behind.

The boy stared her in the eye and pushed his hand towards her.

'You didn't have to come after me,' Ylva said. 'This isn't my fault.'

Bron dropped the reins and turned his back on her.

'Leave with me and live,' Cathryn said. 'Or stay here and die. It's your choice.'

Ugh. More choices. Ylva looked around, wishing Geri was there for her to put words in his mouth. Where was he? It was so much easier when she had him to—

Even as she wished for him, Geri appeared from the bracken and trotted to her side, pressing his muzzle into her open hand. He brought with him a wave of relief and comfort that flooded through her.

This time we should go with her. Please.

Ylva glanced back at the flames moving to and fro among the trees.

There are too many of them to fight.

Ylva looked down at Geri's dark, pleading eyes then let out a sigh. 'You're right.' She took the reins and climbed up, speaking softly to the horse. The animal settled to her quickly and Ylva brought it round to where Cathryn was struggling to hoist herself into the saddle. She was in a lot of pain, but Bron came to her aid, giving her enough support to climb up.

Cathryn took a moment to catch her breath, then looked down at Bron. 'The girl will come with me. We'll make our way to Seatun; it's probably safest that way. We'll be a day, maybe two; depends how long it takes to shake them off. We'll meet there.'

Bron wasn't happy about it; that much was clear from his expression.

'Seatun,' Cathryn repeated. 'Show me you heard.'

Bron nodded and touched his ear. *Yes, I heard.*

'Good. And mess up your tracks. Change direction. Confuse them. You know how to do it better than anyone.' Cathryn turned her horse north-west and nudged it forward as Bron melted back into the forest.

Ylva took one last look behind her at the flames flickering through the trees before she followed.

The three-fingered man was out there somewhere.

17

Wild Music

They rode until the flames were no longer visible. When it was safe, they slowed down and the only sounds were the steady swish and thump of hooves and the huff, huff, huff of the horses' breathing.

Ylva looked down at Geri, then back at the unmistakeable trail they were leaving through the woods. 'Even a blind man would be able to follow us,' she said.

'They'll be moving slower than us,' Cathryn told her. 'They'll be wondering if we have anything planned for them.'

'Planned for them?' Ylva asked.' Like what?'

'A nasty surprise.'

'What kind of nasty surprise?'

'An ambush, maybe.'

'So why didn't you just say that?'

'I thought I did.'

'Oh.' Ylva touched the cut on her face, feeling where the blood had already hardened along it. 'But we're not going to ambush them?'

'The best thing we can do is put as much distance between them and us as we can.' With the reins in her left hand, Cathryn held her right arm close to her chest for support, but every time she moved in the saddle, she winced with the pain of it.

'Why?' Ylva asked. 'Why don't we ambush them? We could lie in wait for them and—'

'And what? Attack them with bad language? Or maybe we could throw snowballs at them, how about that?'

'I don't think snowballs would do much good.'

'I didn't actually mean . . . oh never mind.'

'I have an axe and a knife,' Ylva said. 'And you have the sword and your axe.'

'Do you have any idea how many raiders are back there? There might be twenty or thirty of them. Strong and battle-hardened warriors. Do you really want to face that?'

'There might only be three,' Ylva said.

'We still wouldn't have a chance. Things almost never go how you plan them.' Cathryn shook her head. 'I can't decide if your head's empty north of your mouth or if you're just one tough little girl. Or maybe you're both.'

'I'm not little. And I have to be tough.'

'Well, maybe that's true, but sometimes we have to know when it's time to stop being tough and start being smart. And this is one of those times, child. It's hard to lay an ambush when you don't know how many fighters are on your trail, and it's hard to hide when you have a trail as wide as the Tine River leading to where you're hiding. Add the fact that my fighting abilities were halved the moment my right arm broke, and you've never killed a man before—'

'How difficult can it be?'

'How difficult can it be?' Cathryn said it like she couldn't believe it. 'Child, there's no chance of us laying an ambush and not coming out of it dead. A wise warrior chooses her battles carefully. Don't go into a fight you can't win. Our best hope is to confuse our tracks, pray for more snow, and get as far away from those men as we can.'

'You mean go to Seatun.'

'Yes, child. We go to Seatun.'

'But isn't it a Saxon village? Is that safe for me? I'm a Dane.'

'There's no one in Seatun to hurt you.'

'You're sure of that?'

'As sure as my arm is broken.'

Ylva watched Cathryn and chewed her lip as she tried to contain her frustration. She considered pressing the idea of an ambush, but could see that Cathryn wasn't going to budge on it. And she was probably right, anyway. Maybe it *was* a bad idea.

She would just have to wait. Her time would come.

⇒⇒⇒———→

They didn't talk for a long while. There wasn't much to say, so they kept on riding through the night. If they found rocky ground, they used it, and they changed direction often, doing what they could to disguise their tracks. But the longer they stayed on horseback, the more uncomfortable Cathryn looked. For the first time since their escape, Ylva really took notice of how bad she was; the way she grimaced every time her horse moved, the way she cradled one arm with the other. The way she hung her head and her face glistened with sweat, despite the cold.

'She looks bad,' Ylva said to Geri, who was still trotting alongside the horse. His mouth was open, his tongue lolling to one side.

You need her. You should do something to help her.

Geri was right; she did need Cathryn. Ylva knew something about living wild, but she didn't know this country. She didn't know how to navigate the land like Cathryn did. If she wanted to survive the forest and find her way to Seatun, she needed Cathryn to get her there. For now, she was on the run from the three-fingered man, but that would change. And if she couldn't persuade Cathryn to help her kill him, maybe there was someone in Seatun who would help her.

'We need to do something with that arm,' Ylva said.

'Huh?' Cathryn raised her head. 'What's that?'

'Your arm. We need to do something about it.'

'Broken is broken, child. There's nothing can be done for it.'

'Broken or not,' Ylva said, 'we can make it more comfortable.'

Cathryn grunted as if to say nothing would make it better.

'One time at home, I fell from a tree and hurt my

arm,' Ylva said. 'I was trying to pick an apple for Mother, pretending they were Idun's apples, and I wanted to get the juiciest one I could find so she could live for ever. Only thing is, the best apples grow on Ragnar Olavson's tree, and the juiciest of them was right at the very top. Ragnar is a mean old farmer who lives close to our village. He always leaves his dogs to guard his trees, but they never growl at me. Dogs like me. So I climbed the tree, all the way up, and I had my hand on the best apple when Ragnar saw me. He shouted at me for stealing, and it gave me such a surprise I slipped and fell. Hit every branch on the way down.' Ylva couldn't remember the pain exactly – your body has a way of making you forget pain like that – but she could imagine it. 'I thought I was going to die,' she said. 'And maybe if Ragnar Olavson had his way, I would've done.'

'Good story,' Cathryn said. 'But it hasn't helped me.'

Mother had checked Ylva's arm and told her it wasn't broken. It had hurt, though, so she put it in a sling to take the weight off it and let it rest. Having it supported like that had been a big relief. Perhaps it would be the same for Cathryn.

Ylva turned to check the contents of the goatskin bags that hung over the saddle behind her. One was stuffed with cloth-wrapped provisions, so she pulled out a bundle and unwrapped it.

'Salted fish will be good for my empty stomach, but not so good for my arm,' Cathryn said.

Ylva ignored her and shook the shrivelled strips of dry, salted fish into the goatskin bag. She refastened the ties then opened out the cloth and decided it was big enough. Trusting the horse to keep moving on, she let go of the reins and knotted two corners of the cloth together.

'A sling,' Cathryn said. 'Maybe you're not so empty-headed after all. Smart and tough is a good combination for a young warrior, you should work harder at it.'

Ylva leant over and passed the sling to Cathryn, who struggled to put it over her neck and tuck her right arm inside.

'Not bad.' Cathryn was out of breath by the time she was finished. 'But you didn't tell me; did you get the apple? For your mother?'

'No.' Ylva reached to her belt and unfastened the small pouch she had taken from the hut. 'I have henbane seeds. If we stop, I can make a paste to put on your arm and—'

'We can't stop here.' Cathryn shook her head. 'Anyway, I've seen people go mad from that stuff. The sling will be enough for now.'

'But I know how. Mother taught me.'

'Save it for another time.'

'Fine.' She refastened the pouch to her belt and took the reins once more.

'The sling is good though,' Cathryn told her. 'Your mother would be proud of you.'

Ylva began to feel that if they kept riding and riding until the end of time, all she would see was trees and snow in the never-ending night.

'It's like Fimbulvetr has arrived,' she said. 'The endless winter before Ragnarök. That's when all the worlds will face their final battles, you know; when Fenrir will swallow Odin, and Thor will kill the World Serpent, just like I'll kill the three-fingered man.'

'As I remember it, Thor dies,' Cathryn said.

'I don't care.' Ylva rolled with the movement of the horse as she watched Cathryn. 'You know our gods, but you look and sound like a Saxon. What are you? A Saxon or a Dane?'

'Why can't we just be people?'

'Because I'm a Dane. A Viking.'

'Of course you are.' Cathryn brought her horse to a stop.

'And you're a Saxon.' Ylva stopped beside her.

Cathryn closed her eyes and turned her head slowly from side to side.

'What are you doing?' Ylva asked. 'Why have you stopped?'

Cathryn held up a hand, telling Ylva to hush.

'But—'

'Shh! I'm listening.'

Ylva frowned and they sat in silence. The horses nickered, and chewed the bits between their teeth. Ylva watched her own breath and hugged herself to keep warm. Geri sat patiently beside her horse, panting and licking his lips to catch his drool.

'All right.' Cathryn opened her eyes. 'It's time to do some more work. We need to split up and confuse the tracks.'

'Split up?' Ylva scanned the never-ending darkness of the forest.

'It's just for a short time,' Cathryn said. 'You ride that

way.' She pointed to her right. 'I'll go the other.'

Ylva looked into the trees and dug one hand into her long hair. She gripped a handful and tightened her fist. The hair pulled at her scalp.

'Don't be afraid, child.'

'I'm not afraid. I'm . . . concerned.'

'I'm pleased to hear it.' Cathryn touched a finger to her ear. 'Hush now and listen.'

Ylva waited in silence but when Cathryn didn't speak again she said, 'Listen to what?'

'To the forest. To the world. I want you to take your hand out of your hair and listen to it all. Start here,' she tapped her chest, 'and work your way outwards.'

'How can I listen from here?' Ylva lowered her hand and put it over her heart. 'That doesn't make any sense.'

'Just do it, child. Close your eyes and do as I say. For once in your life do something without questioning it.'

'Are you serious?' Ylva stared at Cathryn for a long moment but when the woman didn't reply, she sighed heavily and rolled her eyes. They were wasting time; the riders chasing them might have followed them this far and could be close by. 'I don't hear anything.'

'That's because you're afraid. Listen through your fear.'

'I told you, I'm not afraid. I'm concerned.'

'Just do it. I'm trying to teach you something. Your dog can do it too, if it makes you feel safer.'

'What do you mean by that?'

'Nothing, I just . . .' Cathryn shook her head. 'Nothing.'

Do it. Close your eyes and I'll do it too.

Ylva glanced at Geri sitting beside the horse. 'All

right.' She took a deep breath and closed her eyes.

'Good. What do you hear?' Cathryn asked.

'My own heart,' Ylva said. 'And the horses.'

'And beyond that?'

Ylva turned her head. 'The wind. Like voices whispering. I hear . . . I think branches rubbing together.'

'Further?'

'Trees creaking. It's a sad sound, as if they're crying. I can hear snow falling from the branches, too, and something small moving in the bracken. Rabbits maybe, or birds.'

'There's something else, child, can you hear it? It's like music.'

'I hear it. Is there a river close by?'

'Good.' Cathryn nodded. 'Open your eyes. The water you hear is a beck. One that becomes a river. Lucky for us it hasn't yet frozen over, and it's wide enough and deep enough to be our friend. I want you to keep riding until you come to it. When you do, take your horse into the water and turn upstream. Move against the current and keep going until you reach a rock that looks like an open hand.' Cathryn held up her good hand, fingers outstretched to demonstrate. 'I'll meet you there.'

Ylva looked in the direction she was to ride. 'What if I miss it?'

'You won't. Even a blind man riding a three-legged goat couldn't miss that beck. And practise your listening. Learn to do it without stopping, without closing your eyes.'

'What about the rock? What if I—?'

'It's bigger than a hall, child. You'd have to be blind

and stupid to miss it on a night as clear as this.'

'But . . .' Ylva put her hand into her hair again and pulled on it.

'You'll be fine,' Cathryn told her. 'I promise. But we're wasting all the time we just made for ourselves if we sit here arguing. Find the beck and follow it to the hand-shaped rock. I'll see you there in two hours.' Cathryn turned her horse and rode away without looking back.

Ylva watched her and considered going after her. Suddenly she didn't feel quite so tough any more. Maybe this was Cathryn's way of getting rid of her.

'Do it, child,' Cathryn called back. 'Do it now.'

18

The Giant's Hand

*Y*ou think she's left us, don't you? That she won't come back.

'We have to be ready for that.' Ylva didn't want to frighten herself, but she had to be prepared for what might come.

But we're going to do what she told us, aren't we? Find the beck and follow it to the hand-shaped rock?

'Yes.'

I don't think she was lying. Geri trotted alongside the horse, with his nose to the ground and his ears swivelling to pick up the sounds of the forest. *She'll meet us. I trust her.*

'Oh Geri.' Ylva sighed as her suspicions deepened. This was a trick. Cathryn had sent her this way so the half-skulls would follow her, leading them away from Cathryn and Bron. Ylva was a decoy and Cathryn was—

I see it. Geri interrupted her thoughts, racing ahead, gliding through the bracken. *There.*

Ylva saw it too; something glistening among the trees ahead, and as she came closer, the song of water on stone grew louder. A sweet, fresh smell touched the breeze.

She wasn't lying about the beck.

'It doesn't mean we can trust her.'

I trust her.

'You're a dog; you trust everyone.'

The beck was a dark and bloated serpent sliding through the snow. Its scales were ripples and eddies glittering with reflected light from the stars and moon, glimmering where it frothed around black rocks. The beck's music, and its wild, crisp scent, reminded Ylva of the river where she and Mother went to spear fish in the summer. Mother was always better at it. Her white feet sliding across the hard pebbles in the shallows. The flash of scales catching the sunlight. The splash of the spear cutting through the water. They would never do that again. Never—

Stop thinking about her.

'I know.'

There was no valley or ditch, no slope down to the water in front of her, just the coil of the beck winding level with the ground. It wasn't wide at the point where Ylva reached it, but she judged it too wide for a grown man to clear in one leap, and there was no telling how deep it was until she encouraged her horse into the water and saw it reach his knees. It would be cold, but the horse didn't complain, and neither did Geri, who splashed straight in and followed them, keeping his head high above the surface.

She travelled slowly. It was a dangerous trick, riding the horse through the water, not knowing what was beneath the surface, but Ylva saw the sense in it. Her trail would disappear when it reached the beck. Anyone tracking her would have to decide upriver or down. There was little chance of finding prints in the riverbed, rocky as it was, and any sign she might leave would be washed away in moments.

'This is good,' she said aloud. 'We'll be like ghosts.'

Ylva kept her wits about her. She focused her full concentration on the task of watching the stream ahead, looking for hidden dangers, and keeping her eyes open for the hand-shaped rock.

Cathryn said you couldn't miss it.

'Then let's make sure we don't.' Ylva's confidence was growing. Cathryn hadn't lied about the beck, and they were progressing towards the place where they would meet her. Perhaps they wouldn't be alone for much longer.

Her ears were filled with the *swoosh-swoosh-swoosh* of the horse moving through the water, but she stopped from time to time to listen as Cathryn had shown her.

To really listen.

Further upstream, the bank to her left became rocky and rose sharply so it towered above her head. The water deepened and widened, and the serpent-like beck became stronger as it washed around the horse. Soon the water was high enough to reach the animal's shoulder.

Ylva lifted her feet to avoid soaking her boots and felt sorry for the horse, its legs and belly in the icy river. She took him into the shallows where it was easier for both him and Geri. She was tempted to give them some respite by moving up on to the bank, but that would be a mistake. If she left the water, she would leave a trail.

And a trail could be followed.

⋙⟶

Cathryn had been right; when she arrived, there was no mistaking the hand-shaped rock. The bank on one side of the river had become steeper the further they travelled, and Ylva had been afraid she would miss the meeting point, but now she knew she was in the right place. The trees were sparse on the left bank, the land too craggy for them to grow, and the moon shone like a spotlight on five enormous, jagged fingers. It was as if a rock-giant had punched his fist from beneath the earth and opened his hand to reach skywards. If Thor was there, Ylva thought, he would swing his hammer and break it to pieces.

The river sang and the forest moaned in the wind, but there was no sign of Cathryn – or any other rider, for that matter.

Ylva urged the horse out of the water and on to a flat rocky shelf that formed the riverbank below the fingers. The shelf was sheltered enough that it was covered in only a dusting of snow. There was debris there, sticks and branches discarded by the river serpent when the water had swollen and receded after heavy rain.

Geri shook himself and sat watching the forest. Ylva waited for the horse to settle before she listened once more. Again, she heard nothing but the river's song, and the forest's complaints.

Ylva didn't like to sit idle. At home, she was never without a job to do. Being still gave her mind room to wander more than was good for her. She chewed her lip and thought about Mother, and wished they'd never come to this country. At home she hadn't had much, but here she had nothing at all. She was cold and hungry and miserable. She would have given almost anything for a warm fire, a dry roof, and a bowl of Mother's plum pudding. Thick and sweet, it was good enough to make almost anything feel better. Sometimes she and Mother would sit in the long grass on the dunes and eat it while watching the sea. Sweet-smelling steam would embrace them as they dreamt about sailing away to somewhere new, just the two of them. But she had never thought it would be like this.

Not like this.

She felt the ache in her heart and tried to bury it, but no matter how deep she pushed it, the pain was always just below the surface.

How long have we been waiting? Geri looked up at the moon.

'Not long. It probably feels like longer.' Ylva turned and studied the fingers of rock standing proud behind her. 'I'm sure this is the right place. Does that look like a hand to you?' She held up her own pale hand towards the rocks and stretched out her fingers to imitate their shape.

'Do you really think she's coming?' Ylva looked down at Geri, but he continued to stare at the sky through the trees. 'Or do you think she sent us in this direction and went in the other to meet that boy. Maybe I should never have trusted her.'

The thought of it cut through Ylva like a cold knife. Without Cathryn, she was stranded. Lost. Left in the forest to die.

19

Shelter

Ylva stood where overhanging rocks sheltered the ground from snow. Geri crouched beside her, huddled and shaking. His fur was damp and matted, and the sight of him made Ylva uneasy, though she didn't understand why. He looked like the mangy, starving dogs in the village at home — the kind whose owners didn't care about them.

So now we wait for Cathryn.

'It doesn't matter if she doesn't come.' Ylva was already preparing herself for the worst; persuading herself she would cope. 'We'll stay here long enough to get warm and dry, the horse can rest, then we'll go.' As she spoke, she searched among the sticks on the rocky shelf until she found one that was thick, and as tall as she was. 'We'll look for this village Cathryn mentioned.

Seatun. Maybe we can find someone there to help us.'

We need a fire.

'No. If the three-fingered man is out there, he'll see it.' She remembered the way he had sniffed the air like an animal. 'Or smell it. We'll have to find another way to get warm. Come on; this way.'

The land itself would provide much of the shelter she needed, so Ylva and Geri climbed up from the shelf and encouraged the horse to follow.

'This is a good place.' Ylva found a spot between two of the giant fingers, where the black rock stretched up on two sides, standing proud in front of a dark cliff that offered protection from behind. Inside the web of the two fingers, there was only a light dusting of snow on the ground – a good sign that the wind blew mainly from the back.

Sheltered from the worst of the weather, Ylva brought the horse across the entrance for added warmth and protection. The horse carried a sheepskin bedroll, two bags, and a large folded fur behind the saddle, so she dried him with the fur, laid it over his back, and hobbled him to stop him from moving away.

She and Geri retreated to the furthest corner of their rocky shelter and Ylva searched the bags the horse had been carrying.

'I wish I had my satchel,' she said as she opened the first bag. 'It had everything we need.'

I wish Mother were here.

The goatskin bags from the horse provided enough to replace what Ylva had lost. There was hard cheese, bread, smoked meat, and dried fish. A clay pot, small enough to fit in her palm, contained strips of charcloth made from touchwood fungus boiled in urine. It was still smouldering – and would continue to do so for days – so she could use it to light a fire when the time was right. There was also a waterbag, a small pouch of salt, three silver coins, and five iron arrowheads.

When Ylva had made a mental inventory of everything, she rechecked and recounted it three times, then returned it to the bags and secured them.

'So now we wait for Cathryn.' She pulled the axe from her belt and sat with her legs crossed. 'If she comes.' She gripped the axe close to the top of the handle and, using the sharp blade, began to whittle a point at one end of the stick she had brought up from the ledge.

Shhkk. Shhkk. Shhkk.

'I can tell you a story if you like,' she said.

Geri whined and curled beside her, pushing against her thigh.

'Mother told it to me one day when we were sitting on the dock with our feet in the water, and the sun on our shoulders.' Ylva continued to carve as she spoke, imagining the warmth of the day, and the ripples glittering on the surface of the sea. 'I was dipping my finger into the water and drawing pictures on the wood but the heat kept drying up my patterns. You were lying in the sun, curled up exactly like you are now. You loved days like that.' Ylva had loved days like that, too; lazy days when she wasn't breaking her back in the fields or wearing down her fingers at the loom. She would let the sun drain her energy and then she would lie with her face on Geri's stomach and feel the rise and fall of his breath as she lost herself in the smell of his warm, soft fur.

But those days were gone now, so Ylva pushed the image away and began to tell the story of Signy, who married the wicked and jealous King of Gautland. 'Do you know it?' she asked Geri, but if she knew it, then it meant he knew it, and she was going to tell it anyway, just to pass the time and to remind herself of her purpose.

Ylva took a deep breath and told how the King of Gautland hated Signy's family, especially her brother Sigmund, who refused to sell him the sword he had won from Odin. 'So when Signy's father and her ten brothers arrived in Gautland to visit her, the Gauts attacked them.' Ylva's words were hardly more than a whisper. 'There was a fierce battle but the King of Gautland won in the end, killing Signy's father and all his men. Signy pleaded for her brothers' lives, of course, what else would she do?' Ylva paused and glanced up at Geri, who sighed deeply.

'She begged the wicked king to lock them up instead of killing them, and he agreed, but really it was a lie; just a way to make them suffer even more. He built stocks from a huge tree trunk and kept the ten brothers trapped in the forest. And every night, the King's mother turned into a wolf and came to them, and every night she ate one of the brothers; killed him and swallowed him up while the others watched. She did it every night until Sigmund was the only one left.

'By then, Signy hated the King as much as anyone

could hate a person – maybe even as much as I hate the three-fingered man – and she was desperate to get revenge on him, but first she had to save her brother Sigmund, so she persuaded a servant to go into the forest and smear honey on Sigmund's face. That night, when the she-wolf came, it tasted the honey and started to lick it all off. And when its disgusting tongue went into Sigmund's mouth, he bit right through it. The wolf died of shock and Sigmund broke free. Signy's last and favourite brother survived.' Ylva stopped whittling and looked at Geri.

'You're quiet,' she said.

It's cold down here. And dark.

'Don't leave me.' Ylva could hardly bear to see him so bedraggled. His coat was dull and the sparkle had gone from his eyes.

Forget about me and finish the story.

'All right.' She cleared her throat. 'So . . . much later, Signy had a son who was strong and brave, and Signy knew he would get revenge for her as soon as he was big enough. He spent a lot of time with Sigmund, having adventures in the forest and fighting battles. One time they even put on wolfskins and became wolves for ten days, but when Signy's son was finally ready, he and Sigmund sneaked into the King's hall at night and set the whole place on fire. They burnt everyone alive. Everyone. Even Signy. But at last, after all that time, and all that waiting, she got her revenge.'

It was a good story, Ylva had always liked it, and when she finished telling it, she bit her lips and tried not to think about Mother.

Mother always told the best stories.

The sound of whittling echoed from the rock walls. *Shhkk. Shhkk. Shhkk.*

'I know what you're thinking.' Ylva watched Geri lying still beside her. 'You're thinking that Signy died in the fire too, so what good came of it? That's what you're thinking.'

Geri raised an eyebrow.

'Or maybe you're thinking, why didn't Signy just kill the King herself? She could have done it when he was asleep. That would have been easier. She could have taken a knife and—'

Maybe she wasn't strong enough.

Ylva stopped whittling, and all was quiet.

Are you strong enough?

'Yes.' Ylva stood to test the spear she had made, thrusting it forwards against an invisible foe. 'When the time comes, I'll be strong enough.'

She went to the horse and stroked his neck as she looked down at the river.

'If anyone passes below, there's a good chance they won't notice we're here,' she said as she went back to Geri and leant the spear against the rock. She sat down and practised grabbing it a few times, to be sure she was prepared for an attack, then she laid the axe beside her and watched Geri.

Huddled and unmoving, he wasn't much more than a dark shape. The damp, musty smell of his fur was growing worse; as if he had crawled out from beneath the ground.

'I know how to survive,' Ylva said. 'And I have food

and shelter. I'll be safe until daylight, then I'll find my way out of the forest – see if I can find this place Seatun that Cathryn told me about. But until then I need to be alert.'

Cathryn will come.

'I don't think so.' Ylva closed her eyes and listened to the forest.

The river was the most dominant sound, but when Ylva listened deeper, she heard bird calls and small animals scurrying in the trees. She became one with the forest around her, letting herself be a part of it. She needed to feel at home here, and for a moment she did. When her whole being was focused on the sounds around her, there was nothing else to think about, nothing else to muddy her feelings.

But her concentration was broken by the chink of tack. The soft *swish-swish* of something moving in the river. A sniff. Someone was coming.

Ylva froze. Her eyes widened. Her mind muddled.

The three-fingered man.

He had found her.

Move, she told herself. *Move!*

Her throat was dry and her heart was pounding. Every muscle cramped.

Fight! her mind screamed at her. *Survive!*

And then she was moving. The fear was not gone, but the paralysis was broken. She snatched up the spear and crouched with one knee on the ground, the other supporting her elbow as she aimed the point of the spear towards the opening of her shelter. She ignored Geri, huddled at the back like a ghost, and she listened.

The rider was approaching from her right. Ylva was certain there was just one. The gentle clink of tack and the unmistakeable swish of a horse moving through the shallows did not overlap in the way they would with multiple riders.

When the sound stopped, Ylva waited a while. Her horse snorted and turned in the shelter's entrance, looking down at the water to see what was there. As it did so, Ylva inched forwards, pointing the spear ahead of her. Someone was there. They hadn't passed by, but had stopped in the river beside the rocky shelf just below her. Ylva prepared herself for a fight. If it was anyone other than Cathryn down there, she would thrust the spear and—

'This is becoming a habit.'

Ylva stared.

'You pointing a weapon at me, I mean. It's becoming something of a habit, don't you think?'

Ylva had convinced herself she wouldn't see Cathryn again. She had been sure she would have to survive alone. But when she saw Cathryn, an unexpected feeling of relief flooded over her like a winter wave on the open sea. She wasn't alone any more.

'I see you made yourself a spear. Very resourceful.'

Ylva looked at the spear, then at Cathryn.

'And you seem to have settled yourself in for the night, but we don't have time to be playing games.'

'Games? I'm not playing games. I would have killed you.'

'I don't doubt it. It was just an expression.'

'Oh.' Ylva lowered the weapon. Her hands were

shaking, and not just with the cold. 'I thought you weren't coming.'

'That I'd leave you out here on your own?'

'Yes.'

'That says more about you than it does about me.' Cathryn steadied her horse. 'Well, you picked a good spot I suppose. It's well protected.'

'We could stay here for the night. Get some—'

'No. We have to keep moving. I know a better place further upriver. And if you like this place, then you'll love the one I've got in mind.'

Endless Winter

20

Ulfhednar

Ylva packed up the bedroll and the goatskin bags to take to her horse, but Cathryn stopped her from throwing them over its back, ready for the saddle.

'Not there,' she called up to her. 'Put the bags and the fur on my horse; we're going to set yours off that way.' Cathryn pointed to the opposite side of the river. 'If anyone manages to track us through the water, they'll get here and see a trail heading off through the trees in that direction.'

'And if the gods are with us, they'll follow it?'

'Gods have got nothing to do with it, child. It's a good idea, so it'll work.'

Ylva secured everything she could behind Cathryn's saddle, and told Geri to wait on the shelf while she took her horse a little further back downriver.

Once she had gone far enough, Ylva let the animal step out of the water and on to the opposite bank. She leant over to rub his neck. 'Thank you for bringing us this far.' They were losing a valuable horse and he had been good company; she was sorry to see him go.

'Will he be all right?' Ylva turned to Cathryn and raised her voice over the sound of the singing water. A mist had arisen, as if spirits were clawing their way out from the forest floor. It hung over the black rocks and swirled around the horse's fetlocks.

Sitting in the saddle, Cathryn looked enormous compared to the small shape of Geri standing on the far bank, but even from this distance, Ylva could see the dog shivering despite his thick fur. She watched his ghostly face, his wide dark eyes, and felt a great longing to be with him. He felt so far away, as if he were staring at her from the world of the dead.

'He'll have as good a chance as we do,' Cathryn said.

Ylva kept her eyes on Geri. 'What about bears? And wolves?'

'What about them? If that horse can save my life – or yours, for that matter – I'd be happy to send him into a den of wolves.'

'It feels . . . wrong. He brought me all this way. He helped me. He deserves better.'

'He's helping you now, child. Get on with it.'

She's right. Geri watched her from across the river.

'I don't want to.'

Sometimes you have to let things go.

Ylva looked away from him and rubbed the horse's neck again. She whispered goodbye and slapped him hard on the hindquarters. The horse flinched and swished his tail in irritation. He blew through his nose and looked around as if to ask Ylva what she was doing.

'Go!' Ylva waved her arms. 'Go on. Go!'

The horse watched her with disinterest.

'That's the problem with a horse that's accustomed to seeing action,' Cathryn said. 'He doesn't scare easily. Slap him with that.' She pointed to the spear in Ylva's hand. 'That'll do it.'

Ylva hesitated. The horse had brought her safely through the forest, and this was how she was going to repay him?

'Do it, child. Time to go.'

Ylva closed her eyes and brought the flat of the stick down with force. It cut through the cold air with a cruel swish and struck the horse's rump with a hard smack. Immediately, the horse reacted. He let out a sharp complaint and bolted into the mist and snow, skidding through the trees and out of sight.

'Be safe,' Ylva said. 'Please be safe.'

With even more weight in her heart, she watched the horse until he was gone, then used the rocks as stepping stones to return to where Cathryn waited in the shallows by the craggy shelf. Before climbing up behind the Saxon woman, Ylva crouched beside Geri. She was hoping for warmth, but he shivered like a cold-fevered dream. And when she put her face to his fur, longing for that comforting blend of fresh air and woodsmoke, there was only the empty-grave smell of damp, stale earth.

>>>——————→

Ylva had been prepared to be alone, but the forest was less threatening now she was with Cathryn again. She still kept her wits about her, and she wouldn't allow herself to relax, but she was less afraid. There was something else too; Cathryn had met her at the hand-shaped rock as she had promised. Ylva had expected betrayal, but Cathryn had kept her word.

Geri picked his way along the rocks on the riverbank beside them, but every time Ylva glanced down at him, he looked a little thinner, a little slower, and a little more ragged. The dank and musty smell of his fur now lingered in her nostrils, and she hated that it turned her stomach.

She tilted her face upwards to breathe the fresh, sweet air that rose from the flowing water, and rolled with the horse's movement as they progressed upriver. From time to time they stopped and listened, but they heard nothing to make them think the half-skulls were on their trail.

'Who are they?' Ylva scanned the forest. 'The half-skulls?' She glanced at the river snaking into the darkness behind them. 'They said they were hunters of men.'

'Hunters of men,' Cathryn repeated with a sigh. 'That's one way of saying it. There have been a lot of "hunters of men" since the Great Army took Eoforwic last month, and changed its name to Jorvik.'

'The Great Army.' Ylva breathed into the air over her head. 'Led by Ivar the Boneless and Bjorn Ironside. The sons of Ragnar Lothbrok.'

'You know about him?'

'Ragnar Lothbrok? Everyone knows about him. He was the first to raid in England. And now all the Viking warriors from all the towns and villages have crossed the sea to avenge his murder by King Aelle. We came here to settle because the Great Army made it safe.'

'Well it isn't safe yet. Aelle and Osbert are still alive and they're still the kings of Northumbria. They might have stopped fighting each other, now they have a Great Army of Vikings to defeat, but there'll be more blood-shed. You wait.'

'Of course there'll be more bloodshed,' Ylva said. 'The sons of Ragnar Lothbrok will get their revenge. Revenge is important to a Viking.'

'Vikings have come here for more than just revenge, child. You saw that man tied in the forest. You saw how they let him die.'

'They said he was a murderer.'

'He wasn't a murderer; he was a slave.'

'A slave? You mean the half-skulls are slavers? That's what they meant by "hunters of men"?'

'Yes, child. They're taking advantage of the army's success, raiding the villages close to Jorvik, and captur-ing slaves. And you can see how they hunted that man until he was too tired and too cold to live. You've even experienced their cruelty for yourself.'

Ylva thought about Mother lying on the floor of the hut, covered by a blanket. She thought about her buried deep in the cold grave, smelling of damp earth. 'Why would they do that? Why would they kill her? I don't understand.'

'Because they're slavers and they're killers,' Cathryn

said. 'Nothing more than that. Wrong time, wrong place.'

'Wrong time, wrong place?' Ylva whispered the words and looked down at Geri. 'I hate slavers.'

'Bron thinks they're Ulfhednar,' Cathryn said. 'Wolf-warriors. He thinks they get stronger when darkness falls, so he had me paint the symbol on the horses – to ward off evil – but it's a load of rubbish, of course. I heard that Ulfhednar can't be hurt by fire or iron, but Bron's arrows killed them just fine. There's no such thing as monsters and magic.'

'Of course there's such a thing,' Ylva said. 'It makes sense now; I knew there was something strange about them. One of them even had teeth like a wolf. And they howled like . . . you know, they tear their enemies apart and drink their blood?' Ylva shivered. 'And now they're hunting us because we killed their men.'

'There's no magic in it,' Cathryn told her. 'They're just slavers in wolf furs, making noises and sharpening their teeth. Bron's arrows killed them just fine, don't you forget that.'

'Maybe the symbol helped him,' Ylva said, thinking about the quiet, dark-skinned boy. He was wild and quick and strange. 'Why does he speak with his hands?'

'He can say a few words if there's a need for it, but it hurts him like claws in his throat. When I found him, he had that bow in his hands and his neck was cut, and I thought he was dead till he opened his eyes and tried to talk. There wasn't much I could do for him so I took him to the Witch. And before you say anything, child, the Witch is just a healer, there's no magic in it.'

Beyond the rocky banks, the ground levelled out and they passed through a place where the water became shallow again, sometimes hardly even covering the horse's fetlocks. Any shallower, Cathryn said, and it would freeze. There, they were surrounded on all sides by nothing but snow-laden birches standing to attention like soldiers. Too many to count, there were rows and rows of them as if they had been laid in lines by the gods. Further still and the forest grew thicker and darker, closing in on the river, trying to swallow it. Mist swirled through the trees, and the cold was so bitter that Ylva believed she might somehow have travelled into the heart of Niflheim.

'You're not a very good liar.' Cathryn kept her voice quiet, as if she might disturb something dark in the forest. 'And what you told those men about your father made me think you haven't been long in England. You didn't know Dunholm is a Saxon town. So I was thinking about that burnt ship Bron and I saw. The one I told you about. It can't have been there more than a few days, and—'

'My father is dead.' Ylva stopped her and focused on the hypnotic *swoosh-swoosh-swoosh* of the horse's legs in the freezing water. 'He was killed in battle. At home in Denmark.'

'I'm . . . sorry to hear it.'

'He was a great warrior,' Ylva said. 'But he's in Valhalla now. We buried him with his boat and his sword, and we had a great feast to honour him.'

On the banks, the forest grew thick with junipers that brushed against them as they passed, shedding snow and leaving a crisp, sweet scent. Deeper among the trees they entered a dark grove where the water ran black and the world hummed with an unnerving and unnatural silence. The cold air was filled with a thick and rotten smell. There was something ancient and frightening in that place, as if the trees were watching, and the forest could close around them at any moment.

'Did your father really die in battle?' Cathryn's voice sounded flat. Lifeless. 'Was he really a warrior?'

'Of course. Don't you believe me?'

'I'm just trying to understand who you are, child. I want to help you but I know nothing about you. I don't even know your name.'

'You never asked.'

'I did. In the hut where I found you. I asked you then. "I don't care to share it with you" is what you told me.'

Ylva stared at the back of Cathryn's head and hesitated. Telling this Saxon woman her name felt like giving something away. Like losing part of herself. 'My name is . . . Ylva.'

'I don't know that name, does it mean something?'

'It means She Wolf.'

'Huh. That makes sense. A fierce name for a fierce child. Your mother chose it well. And what about your dog? Does he have a name?'

Ylva felt an aching wrench in her heart, and she looked back at Geri falling behind. He was just a shadow of himself now, growing weaker and weaker by the hour.

'You speak to him,' Cathryn said. 'I've heard you.'

Ylva closed her eyes and bit the inside of her cheek so hard she felt it crunch.

'And you see him too, don't you? What was his name?'

Ylva put a hand in her hair and tugged until it hurt. 'Geri. His name was Geri.'

'But you know he's not there, don't you?' Cathryn said. 'You know he's dead; that we buried him beside your mother?'

'Yes,' she said. 'I know.' She opened her eyes and looked back once again, but instead of seeing Geri, she saw nothing but trees and shadow, and she thought about all the times she had pretended to hug him and press her face into his fur.

'In the hut I suspected, but it wasn't until after we rescued you from the half-skulls that I was sure you still see him. It must be hard for you. I can't even imagine it, but—'

'I know he's not there.' Ylva raised her voice and let herself be angry. 'I know. Don't tell me what to do or how to think. Don't tell me to forget him.' She pulled harder on her hair and fought back the tears and remembered how Mother had taken Geri with her into the hut on the mountainside that day. Ylva said he would protect Mother, keep her safe, but now they were both dead, killed by the three-fingered man. 'I don't want to forget him, and I'm going to find that man and make him pay for what he did. He murdered my mother and he murdered my dog, and both of those things are crimes where I come from.'

'I wasn't going to tell you to forget him,' Cathryn said gently. 'I was going to tell you that if you need him, it's all right to keep him alive. Right here.' Her voice was soft as she raised her good hand to touch the side of her head. 'I know you're not like other children, and that's fine. Talk to your dog if you have to. Do whatever you need to do to survive.'

Ylva let go of her hair. 'You don't think it's stupid?'

'No.'

'I like animals. They make me feel calm. Not like people.' Ylva took a deep breath. 'Mother gave him to me when he was a pup, and we've never been apart. It was her idea to give him words. I . . . don't always think the way other people think, and sometimes, if I'm . . . if I'm *concerned* about something, and I don't know what to do, I bite my cheek or pull my hair.'

'I've seen you do that.'

'Well, I used to get so angry I'd hurt myself even worse, so Mother said I should give Geri words if I ever felt like that; if I was confused or scared. As if he was talking to me.'

'I like the sound of her more and more. I wish I'd met her. Geri too.'

The last time Ylva had seen Geri alive was when he and Mother had crossed the snow-covered track, and entered the trader's hut. When she next saw him, he was lying on the dirt floor beside Mother, and she had so wanted it to be untrue. She had tried and tried not to see his broken body. She had tried not to see the blood. And when she had covered him with the blanket, she imagined he had lived; that he was there to keep her company, to be the voice she needed him to be.

But now he had faded from her. He had stepped back into the shadows. Geri was gone, and she had nothing but a black storm of sorrow and revenge.

'It's not stupid,' Cathryn said. 'Not at all. Keep Geri in your head, and your mother in your heart. That way, whenever you need them, they will be with you.'

21

Fenrir

When Cathryn was satisfied they had followed the river for long enough, she steered them away and headed deeper into the forest. But some time after midnight, when Ylva was lost in thought and her eyes were growing heavy, Cathryn pulled hard on the reins and brought the horse to a sudden standstill.

'What is it? Why did we stop?'

Cathryn held up her hand.

'You hear something?' Ylva imagined bloodthirsty Ulfhednar, and wondered if Bron could be right about the men who were hunting them. 'Is it the three-fingered man?'

Cathryn shook her head and tightened her fist, signalling Ylva to stop talking. She cupped her hand behind her ear, so Ylva did the same and leant sideways to look around Cathryn's wide body. As she focused her hearing, she noticed the horse was listening too – both ears were pricked up and turned towards the forest ahead.

And then Ylva heard it.

Perhaps an animal. Perhaps men. Or perhaps it was both. Whatever the sound was, it was coming from the trees ahead of them.

Hindered by her broken arm, Cathryn climbed down from the horse with all the grace of a greedy sow. Ylva almost heard the animal heave a sigh of relief that he no longer had to carry her weight. The enormous woman paused to catch her breath then gestured to Ylva to climb down.

'Is it them?' Ylva whispered when she was standing beside Cathryn. 'Have they found us?' Her insides squeezed tight and a violent shiver ran through her.

The horse was afraid too. It pulled back on the reins as if something was agitating it. His ears turned and focused, all the time staying pricked right up. Cathryn controlled him and hitched his reins to a nearby branch. 'Stay behind me and be quiet.' She drew her sword and headed into the trees on foot.

Ylva tugged the axe from her belt and followed. After a few steps, she glanced back at the horse and saw Geri sitting beside it. Mouth open, tongue hanging to one side, he looked as handsome and strong as she had ever seen him. His fur was clean and smooth and his eyes were bright. He wasn't really there – Ylva knew that – but she would keep him alive and call on him whenever she needed him.

It surprised Ylva that Cathryn moved with hardly a sound. The way she had come down from the horse suggested she was in pain, that she was struggling, but now she was on the ground, she moved like a predator. Ylva walked in her footsteps, placing her own boots into each impression in the snow. When Cathryn crouched, Ylva did the same.

They had crept no more than fifty paces into the forest when Cathryn stopped so suddenly that Ylva almost bumped into her.

Cathryn pointed at a trail by her feet and whispered, 'Bear tracks.' She put her fingers into the deep, clear prints.

'You're sure it's not them? The half-skulls. The *Ulfhednar*?'

'Hush.' Cathryn looked to the right, where the tracks had come from, and ahead where they disappeared deeper into the forest. 'These are fresh.' She leant forward, peering through the trees, then stood and followed the tracks before she stopped again and pointed at a large pile of droppings.

'See that? Definitely a bear. A big one.' Cathryn crouched and touched the dark pile. 'Still warm,' she whispered. 'He's—'

A loud breathy grunt came from close by.

Ylva flinched at the sound of it but Cathryn put out her arm to stop her from moving.

The breathy grunt came again, followed by a rumbling growl. Terror flooded Ylva's veins like molten iron. She had never even glimpsed a bear, but she knew they were feared as much as trolls and dragons. She'd heard about monstrous creatures standing taller than a giant and weighing more than ten men. A horrifying beast that could outrun a horse and take off a man's head with one swipe of its claws. Only the greatest Viking warriors could fight a bear and survive. To her it didn't make any difference if it was Ulfhednar or a bear out there in the forest – she didn't want to meet either. 'We have to go.'

Ylva pushed against Cathryn's arm, wanting to turn and run back to the horse, but Cathryn held firm and glared at her. She shook her head. Running was the worst thing they could do.

So Ylva fought her instinct to flee. She swallowed her fear and stood her ground, waiting for the monster to crash through the forest towards them.

But no attack came. Somewhere in the trees the bear grunted again, then it growled long and hard, and Ylva heard a sharp dog-like yelp. A moment later, there was an eruption of snarling and rumbling, and through the trees Ylva saw the bulk of the fearsome creature. Muscle and fat moving beneath fur that was black in the night. And each time the bear slammed a massive paw on the ground, the earth trembled.

But the bear wasn't coming towards them. It moved to and fro in the forest ahead, first one way, then the other, disappearing and reappearing through the trees. As it backed away, it growled hard and stood on its hind legs, and a second shape blurred in the night; smaller and closer to the ground, but no less ferocious.

Cathryn leant in and put her mouth to Ylva's ear. 'Wolf.'

They stayed where they were, watching, not making a sound. The forest ushered an ice-cold breeze towards them. Heavy flakes of snow began to tumble through the naked treetops. And in the small clearing ahead, the wilderness played out before Ylva's eyes. A bear and a wolf locked in battle.

The wolf was ferocious, like Fenrir himself, but the battle was one-sided. When it leapt at the bear, widening its jaws, the bear lashed out with an enormous paw and smashed the wolf against a nearby tree. The wolf yelped a pitiful high-pitched sound, and crumpled into the deep snow. It tried to get up, but it was broken and beaten, at the mercy of the larger creature. The bear was in a frenzy now; it ran at the injured wolf, trampling and swiping, rising on to its hind legs and bringing its full weight down on the smaller animal, biting at its lifeless body before finally becoming calm and standing over it, steam rising from its nostrils.

The bear stood for a while, as if waiting for its victim to be resurrected. It put its snout closer to the wolf, nuzzling and poking at it, but the wolf lay still so the bear lifted its head and turned in Ylva's direction. Snowflakes settled on its dark fur.

Even from where she was, with the blood thumping in her ears, Ylva heard it sniffing the air.

It knew they were there.

Afraid to make a sound, Ylva held her breath.

On the other side of the glade, the bear reared up on to its hind legs and stood with its back straight, its head towards them. It remained still, like a statue, watching the trees.

Ylva eased the air from her lungs and took another breath. The cold stung her eyes, and when she reached up with her free hand to rub them, the bear thumped back down on to all fours. It raised a massive paw and slapped it hard on the ground, clacking its teeth together and blowing hard through its nose.

When it lowered its head and put back its ears, Ylva knew it was about to attack. She didn't know how she knew, she just knew.

22

Wolf's Blood

The bear came at them like a mighty thunderstorm. It barrelled across the glade in a hurricane of rage and violence.

'Stand your ground!' Cathryn raised her sword. 'Fight hard, Young Wolf, fight for your life!'

Ylva hardly realized she was using both hands to hold her axe at shoulder level, ready to strike. Her entire body was numb with fear. She was not herself any more; she was someone else, floating high above the trees, looking down as the bear thundered through the undergrowth towards her.

Its jaws snapped open and shut, its teeth clattered, and its paws shook the earth.

Ylva braced herself, ready to sidestep and swing her axe as she had seen warriors do while training. She would swing it with all her strength.

But the bear came to a sudden stop. At the nearside of the glade, it skidded to a halt, spraying snow in all directions. It froze in place with its mouth open and its teeth bared. Its chest bellowed in and out with every breath as it fixed the intruders with its small dark eyes.

'Stand your ground,' Cathryn said again.

The bear snorted loudly through its nose.

Ylva stayed as she was. She wasn't sure she could move even if she wanted to. She was frozen with fear, the three of them locked in an impossible showdown.

The bear snapped its yellowed teeth again and again, a sticky wetness of gore glistening on its muzzle. It was hard for Ylva not to imagine her own body caught in those terrible jaws. Each of its finger-length teeth would punch through her skin and crack her bones as easily as she could snap a twig.

'It's trying to scare us,' Cathryn said.

'It's working.'

The bear snorted and lowered its head, preparing to charge again, but before it could move, Cathryn let out a long, loud battle cry. Ylva had heard the shield-maidens making such a noise, and Cathryn did it as well as the best of them. A cry like that would strike fear into enemies on the battlefield. Seeing a horde of screaming warriors running at you across a field, with their axes and spears flashing, could change the whole course of a fight. Enemies sometimes even turned and ran away, but the bear hardly even flinched. It paused for no longer than a second before it charged straight at them.

Ylva thought it impossible that something so big and

so heavy could move with such grace and speed. She'd hardly even had time to register that the bear was moving before it was almost on top of her.

All she could see was bristling fur. All she could hear was thumping paws and mashing teeth. All she could feel was the ground shaking and the wind rushing at her. The enormous beast was going to trample right through her, toss her into the air and—

'Move!' Cathryn's shout brought Ylva to her senses, and they twisted in opposite directions as the bear reached them, jaws snapping together. It swiped with one paw, stumbling as it skidded past through the bracken, but Ylva had moved well clear.

Heart pounding like Thor's hammer, her vision flared white with fear and relief. But when she looked across at where they'd been standing, she saw that Cathryn must have lost her footing as she turned, probably unbalanced by her broken arm, and was now lying on her back in the snow, struggling to get up.

Close by, the bear was already turning towards her, moving in for the kill.

Ylva had to do something. She had to do *something*.

So she let out a battle cry. It was high-pitched and pathetic compared to Cathryn's. It burnt her throat like she had swallowed hot sand, but it was enough to attract the bear's attention.

The beast turned its massive bulk and looked at her across the top of the undergrowth. It huffed and clattered its teeth and broke into a loping run. The ground shook with every step. Tree branches snapped as it passed, and the breath from its nostrils blew warm and rank, but Ylva waited until the last moment. She waited.

And waited.

And waited.

And struck.

It was more luck than skill, but as the bear reached her, Ylva twisted away from it and swung her axe at its enormous head. She landed a fierce blow that shuddered up her arm as if she had struck a chunk of iron.

Dazed and surprised, the bear stumbled as it tried to turn towards the cause of its pain, but it lost its footing and thumped head first into the gnarled trunk of a thick oak tree. The tree trembled, snow cascading from its branches, and the bear collapsed in a bundle. But it wasn't down for long. Before Ylva had time to help Cathryn, the bear struggled to its feet and stepped back. It shook sense into itself, turning its head in confusion, searching for its prey.

Ylva stood with her bloody axe raised, torn between two thoughts; escape while the creature was confused, or attack again and keep on attacking until it was dead.

So she attacked.

She ran at the bewildered beast, screaming and swinging her axe, striking at it wherever she could. She shouted so hard she thought the veins might burst in her head. She made sounds she didn't know she could make.

The bear turned in a circle, huffing and clacking its teeth, disorientated by the chaotic attack. Ylva didn't let up; she rained down blow after blow on the bear, sometimes striking flesh, sometimes bone, and sometimes striking nothing but the cold, cold air.

She fought even though her arms ached and her chest was ready to burst. She couldn't give the creature even a moment to recover, so she fought and fought and fought until, 'Oof!' – a powerful blow struck her hard in the chest.

Ylva's lungs collapsed, her breath sucked away, and she was lifted off her feet. For a moment she was airborne and everything was lost, then she landed in the snow with a thump. But her instinct was to survive. It was always to survive. Within seconds, she was on her feet again, drawing breath back into her body, shouting and swinging her axe, but the bear was not to be struck again. With a final roar, it turned towards the glade and thundered away, crashing through the understorey and disappearing from sight.

Ylva continued to shout and swing her axe until long after the bear was gone. She only stopped when Cathryn came close and said, 'Child.'

Ylva whipped around and raised her axe. There was blood on her face and fingers. The leather-wrapped handle of the axe was slippery in her grip, and the snow around her was splattered.

'It's gone.' Cathryn reached out a hand, but stopped short of touching Ylva.

Their breath steamed between them with every well-earned lungful.

'Gone?' Ylva said when she found her voice. 'You're sure?'

Cathryn nodded.

'Will it come back?' Her whole body was shaking.

'Would you?' Cathryn's face cracked into a smile. 'Would you come back with such a dangerous child screaming at you?'

'What's so funny?'

'Nothing.' Cathryn's smile broadened. 'It's not funny at all. We nearly died, but . . . You.'

'Me? What about me?'

Cathryn chuckled. 'Seeing you battling the bear. A young pup and a fully grown bear.'

'I'm not a pup.'

'But just a young wolf,' Cathryn chuckled. 'A she wolf. If only you could have seen your face! The determination. I've never seen anyone so fierce.' Cathryn put back her head and laughed. 'Maybe you do have the heart of a warrior. If it wasn't for you, I'd probably be dead.'

'Why is that funny?'

Cathryn ignored the question and allowed herself to laugh away the fear and the adrenalin. She laughed until she could hardly breathe, then she calmed herself and looked at Ylva, who was watching her in confusion. 'You have no sense of humour, child.'

'That's what Mother used to say.'

'Uh-huh, well.' Cathryn wiped her face with her sleeve. 'She was probably right. But what you lack in humour, you definitely make up for in bravery. And your battle cry was pretty good. Your mother would've been proud of you. Geri, too.'

'I hit it.' Ylva looked at the blood on her hands. 'Didn't I?'

'You did. And not just once. Maybe they'll write a

saga about you after all. Ylva the Fearless; the child who fought a bear and won. Maybe it's you who's Ulfhednar. I wouldn't be surprised if you have wolf's blood in your veins.'

23

Mercy

Paw prints were scattered to and fro across the glade. In places, it was dappled with black spots that would look red in any other light. But fresh snow continued to fall like silvery petals, layering a touch of beauty over the cruel evidence of the terrible battle. Soon, any evidence of what had happened here would be buried and gone.

Cathryn stepped into the glade and stopped. From a distance it might have been easy to mistake her for a bear. She remained still, watching the trees, her shoulders moving with each heavy and laboured breath. There was sweat on her brow, and weary bags hung under her bloodshot eyes. Soft flakes settled on her furs.

Ylva stood beside her, scanning the clearing, taking in the scent of soil and bark and something else; something wild and dark. Her gaze settled on the shape of the wolf lying trampled at the base of the tree. She was sure it was dead but, as if to prove her wrong, the creature moved. It lifted its head, trying to turn in their direction. The effort was too much. It whimpered and collapsed back into the snow.

'He's a strong one,' Cathryn whispered, and for a moment they stayed where they were, looking from the wolf to the trees and back again, waiting to see if the bear would return.

'Is it one of them?' Ylva asked. 'The Ulfhednar?'

'A man in the form of a wolf? No, of course not. Wolves are wolves and men are men. There's nothing magic about the half-skulls. Remember what Bron's arrows did to them; you saw it with your own eyes.'

'So it's just a wolf?'

'Yes.'

'Then it's cruel to leave the poor creature like that.'

Cathryn nodded once. They understood each other. There was only one thing they could do for the wolf.

Ylva drew her knife, and went deeper into the glade. Cathryn followed, but when Ylva crouched beside the wounded animal, Cathryn remained standing.

Ylva was almost overcome by the beauty and power of the wild animal lying in the snowy glade. It was larger than she had expected a wolf to be. Far bigger than Geri. Its blood-matted coat was musty with decay, and every wheezing breath released a trickle of stale air. Its narrow body was hollow from hunger but there was something powerful in its presence. There was no doubting the wildness and strength of this beast.

Before she knew what she was doing, Ylva ran her hand along the wolf's body. She had done the same when she found Geri lying lifeless in the hut. The fur was coarse and grainy with dirt, and when she took her hand away, there was blood on her fingers. Ylva wiped it on her breeches, and held her hand over the wolf's head. She hesitated, then gently touched the soft fur between its ears. Ylva kept her hand there as she spoke to the dying creature.

'I'm sorry.' She fought back tears and tried not to think of Geri as she reached around the wolf's neck with her right hand and drew her knife across its throat. It only took one swift cut to finish what the bear had started, and Ylva knelt beside the wolf and stroked its head as its life slipped away.

When it was done, she wiped her blade in the snow and then on her breeches. She ran her hand through the wolf's fur once more.

'You did the right thing,' Cathryn said.

Ylva looked up at the woman standing beside her. She was suffering. The huge Saxon who had barged into the hut last night was a shadow of what she had been. Her skin was pale, her eyes tired.

'Your arm is bad?' Ylva asked.

'Yes.'

'You need to rest.'

'I'll rest when I'm dead.' Cathryn managed a smile.

'That could be sooner than you think.' Ylva looked at the wolf, then at Cathryn. 'You need to rest before you die.'

'Uh-huh, well. As soon as we get to the caves, then.'

Cathryn wiped her face and scanned the glade one more time. 'Look.' She pointed to three small dark shapes a few paces away.

Ylva stepped around the wolf's body and moved closer. Now she understood why the wolf had been fighting the bear.

'It was a "she",' Ylva said. 'A mother.'

'Protecting her pups,' Cathryn agreed. 'No wonder she fought so hard. But she was alone. Without a pack, no wolf could beat a bear. Not even one fighting for her pups.'

The she-wolf had burrowed a den into the base of a hazel thicket. A hidden opening that she would have used to provide warmth and protection for her pups. But it hadn't been enough; the dangers of the forest had been too great for her, and now the bodies of her three pups lay scattered close to the den.

'If we hadn't frightened it away, the bear would have taken them for food?' Ylva whispered.

'It's a bad winter, and getting worse. Everything's hungry, child, and that includes you and me and the people following us.' Cathryn looked up at the sky. 'The fresh snow will cover our tracks. Maybe someone up there is looking out for us.'

'I don't think the gods are helping me,' Ylva said. 'It feels more like they're punishing me.'

'Well . . .' Cathryn sighed. 'The bear's gone, I think. Time to move.' She trudged back towards the place where they had left the horse, but as Ylva turned to follow her, she spotted movement by the trees. Her first thought was that the bear had returned, but when she saw the movement again – small and dark against the white snow – she realized what it was. One of the wolf pups had survived the attack.

'Let's go.' Cathryn beckoned for her to return to the horse.

The pup was a different colour from its mother – black, with a teardrop of white on its chest. His coat still had the fluffiness of a pup, and Ylva guessed it was five or six weeks old, but the way it behaved was different from the way Geri had behaved at that age. It was more alert, and steadier on its feet.

'I won't hurt you,' Ylva whispered as she approached.

'What is it? What are you doing?' Cathryn called to her. 'We have to go.'

Ylva ignored her. She got down on her haunches and held her hand out for the pup to smell her fingers, but it jumped back, dodged around her, and ran straight to its dead mother.

Ylva followed it, crouching as the pup huddled against the she-wolf's stomach. It nuzzled against its mother, then sat upright and opened its mouth just enough to show the tip of its pink tongue. Ylva was so engrossed in watching its movements, already forming plans for the pup, that she didn't notice Cathryn approach from behind. The first she knew of it was when Cathryn reached down and grabbed the pup around the neck. She pushed it hard against the ground, grunting as she placed one knee across the squirming animal to hold it in place so her hand was free to draw her knife.

'No!'

Cathryn put the blade against the pup's throat and looked at Ylva. 'It's the kindest thing; it won't survive alone out here.'

'No.' Ylva grabbed Cathryn's wrist, hating the feel of the woman's skin under her fingers. 'Please.'

The pup was small and vulnerable and alone. Its mother was dead, but it was wild and fierce, with a will to survive, and the potential to grow into something special. When she looked at the pup, all Ylva could see was Geri. And herself.

'It will never replace him,' Cathryn said. 'This is a wild animal, not a dog. You can't keep it.'

'You're wrong.'

'How d'you think you're going to kill the three-fingered man?' said Cathryn. 'If you can't even mercy-kill a wolf pup.'

'It's different.' Ylva twisted Cathryn's hand, trying to pull the knife away. 'I can keep him alive. I can look after him just like I looked after Geri when he was a pup.'

'There's no looking after a creature like this. It's a wild animal.' They struggled against each other while the pup squirmed under Cathryn's knee, and when Ylva saw she wasn't strong enough to take the knife, she did the first thing that came into her head; she took advantage of Cathryn's awkward position and the state of her broken arm. She shoved her shoulder into Cathryn with enough force to unbalance her and knock her sideways into the snow.

Cathryn collapsed hard and awkward, grunting with pain as she landed on her right side. Her broken arm took the full weight of the fall. The pup slipped away from her and scrambled back to its dead mother, pressing against her belly for the last of her warmth. Ylva regained her balance and stood up, looking down at Cathryn lying in the snow on her right side. 'I won't let you kill him.'

Cathryn closed her eyes tight and let out a long breath. When she tried to breathe in again, her face contorted with pain. 'I think . . . I'm going to need help.' And there was something in the tone of her voice, in the effort it took for her to speak, that drove an icicle through Ylva's heart.

'What is it?' She stepped back, running a hand into her hair. 'What's wrong? Is it your arm?'

'No,' Cathryn said. 'Worse.' She rolled to her left, holding her hand to her side. 'This is going to be trouble.'

Cathryn's knife was not lost in the snow beneath her. It was right there, piercing her cloak, and firmly embedded in her flesh.

24

A Whole
Lot of Blood

Ylva gripped a handful of her own hair and stared at the knife sticking out from just above Cathryn's right hip. 'You should have just let me save the pup,' she said. 'Now look what you've done.'

'Uh-huh,' Cathryn grunted. 'Or you could have just done as I asked.'

'Are you saying this is my fault?' Ylva's thoughts were a terrible muddle. 'This isn't my fault. It isn't.' She turned away from Cathryn. 'You should've just let me save the pup and then we could go back to the horse and find Seatun and . . .' She balled her free hand into a fist and thumped it against the side of her head. 'This isn't my fault.'

'All right.' Cathryn's voice was quiet. 'It's not anyone's fault. I'm sorry if I sounded angry. This isn't your fault.'

Ylva took a deep breath and turned back to Cathryn. 'Really?'

'Really. But I need you to help me. Can you do that?'

'Yes.' Ylva nodded. 'Yes, I'll help you.' She came closer and dropped to her knees beside Cathryn. 'What can I do?' She reached out with both hands but stopped short of touching the knife handle. 'I can't take it out yet. We have to be ready.'

'Right . . .' Cathryn caught her breath. 'If you take it out, there'll be . . .' She grimaced. 'A whole lot of blood. If there are any more wolves, they'll pick up the scent from halfway across the forest. The bear will smell it from even further. But I'd be lucky not to bleed to death before either of them get here.'

Ylva looked around. 'So what do we do?'

'Get the horse.'

'Horse. Yes.' Ylva jumped to her feet and hurried back to the horse. She unhitched it and led it back to the clearing. She threw the reins over a nearby branch and went straight to Cathryn.

'Now help me sit up.' Cathryn grabbed Ylva's arm with her left hand and gripped hard. 'Do it quick.' She pulled against Ylva who dug her heels into the snow and leant back as Cathryn sat up from the waist. Cathryn sucked in a breath and held on to Ylva to stop from falling back.

After a while, Cathryn opened her eyes and nodded at her. 'Good,' she said. 'Good. Now I need to stand up. You ready?'

'Not really.' Ylva shook her head, making Cathryn

force a smile.

'Me neither,' Cathryn said. 'But here goes.' Once again, she pulled against Ylva and Ylva pulled back with all her weight as Cathryn shifted her legs and manoeuvred into a position from which she could get to her feet.

Once that was done, she wrapped her good arm around Ylva's shoulders and hung her head while she caught her breath. 'Went right under my armour,' she said. 'I can feel it against my rib. Doesn't hurt too much right now, but the pain will come. Later.'

Ylva said nothing.

'All right. Get me on the horse.'

'With that?' Ylva looked at the knife handle, the blade disappearing into the side of Cathryn's cloak.

'For now.'

So Ylva supported Cathryn as she limped to the horse, and she helped her struggle into the saddle, using her shoulder to push her up.

'Now go back and do for that pup,' Cathryn said. 'It's the kindest thing.'

'What? No. I won't.'

'Stubborn child,' Cathryn said. 'I can see that once you've set your mind to something, there's nothing will change it.'

'There's no sense in making up your mind if you keep changing it.'

'Unless there's good reason.'

'That's what Mother used to say.'

'I like her more and more.'

Ylva strode back into the glade where the pup was

still nestled against his mother's stomach. She grabbed him with both hands, tucked him inside her cloak, and returned to the horse.

When she climbed up, Cathryn didn't say anything. She just nudged the horse and they left the glade behind.

25

A Promise

Cathryn rode upright in the saddle. Her breathing was heavy and interrupted by grunts of pain whenever the horse stumbled. Ylva sat behind her, trying not to bump her, afraid to make her pain even more unbearable. She spoke to Cathryn often, mostly to reassure herself that the woman was still conscious.

Inside Ylva's cloak, the wolf pup slept.

An hour or two after they left the dead she-wolf, they came to a narrow ledge that rose up the mountainside. It was precarious to navigate – only just wide enough for the horse – and one wrong step could mean they'd tumble to the ground far below. But they stayed on track and followed it until they were above the tree-tops and Ylva could look out across the forest. Only now did she have a true sense of how vast it was. She was insignificant here; as unimportant as a single leaf fallen from a single tree.

A little higher, and the narrow ledge passed a series of openings just visible in the black rock.

'Barghest Caves,' said Cathryn as she guided the horse into the mouth of the nearest one.

Inside, the damp, moss-covered rock sheltered them from the biting wind. They were well protected from all sides, and the worst of the weather cut across the cave entrance, so there was barely even a dusting of snow on the uneven ground. Ylva had grown so used to the sound of the wind in her ears that the sudden silence of the cave folded around her as if it were solid.

She helped Cathryn down from the horse, settled her on one of the sheepskin bedrolls and threw a rug over her. She was shivering but Ylva couldn't be sure whether it was from the cold or from the knife wound. The woman had done well to make it this far, but she was weakening by the minute.

'Fire,' Ylva muttered under her breath. 'I need to get you warm.' She took the pup from her cloak and put him down, then brought the bags from the horse. The pup sniffed about, but stayed close to Ylva.

Maybe you should forget about the three-fingered man.

'What? No.' Ylva looked up at Geri sitting in the shadows of the cave. She hadn't called for him, hadn't asked for his help, but there he was.

But look what's happened already.

'I'm not giving up,' Ylva said. 'I'm a warrior and I don't give up on anything.'

It wouldn't be giving up. It would be a retreat. Even a Viking shield-maiden doesn't fight battles she knows she can't win.

'I'm not giving up. I made a promise to Mother and . . .' Ylva turned away from Geri. 'And to you.' She chewed the inside of her cheek and muttered under her breath as she busied herself collecting the smaller rocks littered around the mouth of the cave. 'And he took something I want back.' She wouldn't be persuaded to give up on the three-fingered man. She was going to help Cathryn, then she would find him. 'Someone in Seatun will help me.'

She brought the rocks inside and began building them into a low, curved wall close to where Cathryn was lying.

Or maybe no one will help you.

'Then I'll do it myself.' The pup followed Ylva as she worked, scurrying aside when it found itself tangled under her feet.

You're not a warrior.

'Hush.' She pushed the doubt away. 'I fought a bear and won.'

The bear was weak from its fight with the wolf. And men aren't like bears; they're more dangerous — even more dangerous if they're Ulfhednar.

'Get out of my head.' Ylva gripped a handful of her hair. 'I don't need you right now.'

She ignored the voice and continued to work on the wall. When she was finished, she took a piece of narrow rope and fastened it around the pup's neck as a makeshift leash. She weighted the loose end beneath a heavy rock.

'Stay there,' she told him as she left the cave and

ventured down the ledge into the trees. She collected wood from the forest floor, searching for sticks where the snow was thinnest, and brought it back to the cave.

The smouldering touchwood from the pot she had found helped her give life to a small bundle of tinder that she prepared behind the curved wall, and she carefully encouraged it to grow by adding twigs and larger sticks. It was a risk to have the fire, but if she kept it modest, her wall would protect the flames from the wind and hide them from anyone who might pass in the forest below.

The damp forest wood took a while to catch, but once the fire was lit, it had an uplifting effect. Ylva was overwhelmed by how much a simple thing could raise her spirits. It was as if she had lit a small beacon of hope in the cold darkness, and she suddenly didn't care if the fire was visible from the forest below. Her destiny was already decided, so if the gods wanted the three-fingered man to find her, there was nothing she could do to stop it.

The pup was wary of the flames at first, but soon moved as close as his leash would allow. He curled up with his back to the warmth, and watched Ylva peel chunks of moss from the cave walls. When she had enough, she shoved the blade of her knife into the hottest part of the fire, and while the iron heated, she untied the pouch from her belt and sprinkled a pinch of small black henbane seeds on to a flat stone. She was careful not to use too much – too much could be poisonous.

With a round stone, she crushed the seeds into a

powder that she scraped into Cathryn's water bag. She gave it a good shake, and encouraged Cathryn to drink it. 'It'll kill the pain. Mother showed me how.'

'As long as it doesn't kill *me*.' Cathryn took a sip and pushed the water bag away. 'It's time to take it out.'

Ylva nodded. 'I've got everything ready.' She wrapped both hands around the handle. 'Do you want something to bite on?'

'Just pull it out.'

So she did.

Ylva had seen healers tending to wounds before – she had even helped from time to time – but she had never done it all by herself. The knife slid out more easily than she expected. More or less as if she were sliding it out of its own sheath. Straight away, Ylva opened Cathryn's cloak and unbuckled the leather tunic that had been too short to protect her from the blade. She peeled away Cathryn's tunic to reveal the injury, then reached across, took her own blade from the fire and pressed it to the wound.

Cathryn gasped. Her eyes closed and her head fell back against the bedroll, like she'd passed out from the pain.

'There's not as much blood as I thought there'd be.' Ylva wiped it away with one of the cloths from the saddlebag. 'That must be from leaving the blade in.'

She threw the bloodied cloth aside and grabbed a chunk of the moss she'd taken from the cave wall. She pressed it against Cathryn's wound, put a tightly folded cloth on top of it, then tied another around Cathryn's waist to hold it in place.

When that was done, Ylva sat cross-legged beside Cathryn and pulled the loose end of the pup's leash from beneath the rock so he could come to her. He sniffed about, then climbed up and curled into her lap.

'That's good,' Cathryn said, making Ylva look down at her. 'Twice you've patched me up now.'

'Mother showed me how.' Ylva felt the first touch of calm as she stroked the pup's small, warm body.

'And the pain isn't as bad as I thought it would be. I think you'd make a better healer than killer,' Cathryn said.

'Mother knew things. She was a famous healer in our village.'

'Of course she was.'

Ylva looked down at the pup and ran her hand over his head.

'You know, it's not right to put a collar on a wild animal,' Cathryn said.

Ylva touched the rope around the pup's neck. 'It's better than killing him.'

'Maybe. For now. But you'll have to let him go. Nothing should have a collar round its neck – person or beast.' Cathryn looked Ylva in the eye. 'Not a child either.'

'What does that mean?'

'I know what you are, Ylva.'

'You know nothing about me.'

'I know more than you think. I know you're not the killer you want to be. You could have left me back there. In the glade. You could have just left me to die.'

'Would you have left me?'

'No.'

'Why not?'

'Because it wouldn't have been the right thing to do. Isn't that why you helped me? Because it was the right thing to do?'

Ylva thought for a long time. 'Yes,' she said. 'I suppose it is.'

26

Monsters in the Dark

While Cathryn slept, Ylva chewed on strips of dried fish.

Outside, the snow fell over the forest, making her think of the stories Mother had told her on cold dark nights at home. Nights when she'd felt safe and warm, with the fire crackling. Or those told by the wanderers who came to the village and spoke in the great hall.

Sometimes skalds came especially to tell their tales at wedding feasts or at the solstice celebrations. There would be a sacrifice – perhaps one of Jarl Andersen's best horses, or least favourite slaves – then Ylva would help to lay whole roasted pigs and sides of beef on the table. There would be buttered vegetables, stews, sweet fruits and nuts. And endless jugs of strong ale. Everyone would roar and laugh as they listened to tales of the gods, of battles with ogres and monsters, or they would fall silent at the stories of witches and ghosts that roamed the wintry forests. Ylva liked the way the stories made her feel – afraid but safe – but the tale she had enjoyed the most was 'The Death of Bjorn Ivarson'.

The wanderer had arrived in the village one afternoon, asking for food and ale in return for the stories he had collected. As usual, everyone came to the hall to listen and pass the night, and by morning, Ylva had forgotten all of the stories he told – all except for one. The last tale had stuck in her mind. It was a tale of such horror that the wanderer had lowered his voice to a whisper, as if he were afraid even to tell it.

A band of Vikings from the village of Gila had sailed to Northern England three summers ago, to find fame and make their fortune in plunder. They spent many days raiding, burning all the villages and monasteries they came to. Wherever they went, they left a trail of blood in their wake. Monks, farmers, women, children . . . no one was safe from the raiders of Gila. And when the raid was over, the men returned to their ship. The sea god, Njord, watched over them as they made the crossing home in safety and returned to their families.

But there were three greedy brothers on that boat. Three brothers who spent their new-found riches before the winter was even half-done.

And when their riches were gone, they turned their sights on their neighbour, Bjorn Ivarson, who had kept his wealth buried. To make it last, Bjorn had used only a small amount of his treasure, and only when he needed it to buy food and furs for his family. If he returned from a hunt empty-handed, he had silver to buy food from more successful hunters. If he needed furs, or a new axe, he had silver to buy them.

The greedy brothers were so jealous of Bjorn that they spied on him, day and night, to find the place where he had buried his silver. But Bjorn was as cunning as a crow; he suspected the brothers wanted to steal from him so he was careful not to let them follow him to the place where he'd buried his hoard. Many times he led them on a wild chase through the forest until eventually, the brothers became so frustrated and angry they decided to make Bjorn tell them.

One snowy night, the brothers forced their way into Bjorn's home, but Bjorn was no battle-shy Christian monk; he was a Viking. When he woke to find the three brothers standing over his bed, he didn't just lie there and let them harm him. He rolled from his bed, snatched up his sword and fought them. He fought for his life, for his riches, and for the lives of his wife and young sons. But three against one was impossible to win, and soon Bjorn and his family were on their knees.

'Where's your silver?' the brothers demanded.

'I'll never tell you,' Bjorn spat at them. 'But I'll tell you this for nothing; if you kill anyone you see in this room, I will never rest – never – until the gods give me my revenge.'

'We'll see about that.' The brothers killed Bjorn with a single crushing axe blow to his head. They then murdered his wife and sons, so that no one could tell what they had done, and they buried the whole family in the forest behind Bjorn's home.

The mysterious disappearance of Bjorn Ivarson and his family was the talk of the village. His friends had no idea what had happened to him, and the brothers put on a perfect act of innocence. But two weeks after Bjorn's disappearance, an old woman claimed that while she was collecting mushrooms one evening, she saw Bjorn walking in the snowy forest around Gila. Except, he wasn't Bjorn Ivarson any more; he was a draugr. A corpse that lived. She said his eyes burnt red and his skin was black. He left no footprints in the snow, and a rotten smell like bad meat filled the air he passed through. No one believed her, but exactly two weeks and a day after the murder, one of the three brothers was found dead in his home. His eyes were wide and staring, and his mouth was open in a scream of horror.

The two remaining brothers remembered the old woman's story and went straight to Bjorn's grave in the forest. Under the cover of night, they dug it up, but found only the bodies of Bjorn's wife and children.

Bjorn himself was not there.

And as the terrified brothers stared into the grave, Bjorn Ivarson emerged from the forest and tore one of the brothers to pieces with his bare hands.

The next morning, when the villagers found the surviving brother, he was kneeling by the open grave, covered in blood, his mind driven to madness. The only words he ever spoke after that were 'Bjorn Ivarson', but Bjorn's body was never found, and the people of Gila believed that he was still out there in the forest, protecting his buried silver.

Bjorn Ivarson had his revenge.

When Ylva turned and looked out across the trees, she knew there were monsters out there. Not Bjorn Ivarson, perhaps, but monsters nonetheless. And she knew they were looking for her. What she didn't know, was that she would see them again very soon.

27

Freya's Tears

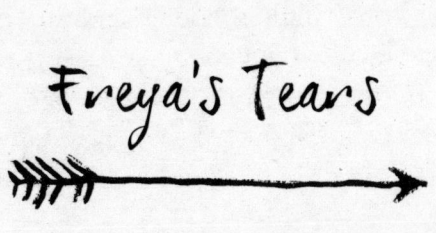

Ylva allowed the pup's leash to slacken so he could explore the cave, but he never went far. He always returned to Ylva's lap where her blankets and cloak shrouded him from the cold. And when he was with her, Ylva held him tight. She ran her hand over his smooth coat, marvelling at the blackness of it. His colouring was much darker than his mother's, and in the firelight it became clear that his eyes were mismatched. One as blue as ice, the other as gold as Freya's tears.

She found comfort in the closeness of the pup, and felt herself relax until exhaustion overcame her. Finally her eyes closed, her head dropped, and she tumbled into a troubled half-sleep.

She was woken by the sound of wolves.

The pup was no longer in her lap. The fire had burnt down to almost nothing, and the cold was fighting its way back into the cave. Out in the forest, a wolf howled again. It was long and terrifying. A sorrowful song that made her skin tighten, and struck the most basic kind of fear into the deepest part of her.

For a few heart-stopping moments, Ylva wondered if the half-skulls had found her. They were Ulfhednar, with the spirit of wolves in their bodies, and they had tracked her the way a wolf would track her. An image leapt into her mind of the first time she had seen the three-fingered man. He had tasted the air and known there was someone hiding in the forest. Did he know she was here now?

Almost too afraid to move, Ylva lowered her hand to the axe at her belt. Her insides were like water, but she had to be strong. She couldn't be afraid. She was Ylva the Fearless.

The pup was standing by the mouth of the cave, the leash taut behind him. He stood with his ears pricked forward and his nose to the air. The horse was a few paces away from him, pulling against his tether, stamping his feet and rolling his eyes in fear. Beside Ylva, Cathryn showed no sign of stirring from her sleep.

The snow was still falling as if it would bury all nine worlds.

Another howl met the first; the two voices twisting together like tendrils of greasy smoke. Then came a third and a fourth, knotting them into a chorus. The pup lost his nerve and trotted back to where Ylva was sitting with her breath held tight in her chest. He pressed against her, so she scooped him up and loosened his leash to put him inside her cloak.

'Don't be afraid,' Ylva whispered. 'Don't be afraid.' She put her finger in the dirt at her feet and drew the same symbol Bron and Cathryn had painted on their horses.

She had no idea if it would help her, but she traced her finger around the shape several times as she gathered the courage to move. When she was ready, she crept over to the horse to settle it. She stroked his neck and spoke to him as the howling continued. 'Just wolves,' she said. 'They're just wolves.'

Ylva stayed with him like that until the sounds softened and faded and the forest was silent again.

28

Wolf-Warrior

The fire dwindled to just a few glowing embers. Ylva was afraid to leave the cave, though she would never admit that to herself, but as the night drew into the early hours of morning, the fire finally died and she was left with no choice. She secured the pup's leash, then took her axe and spear and scrambled down the ledge into the closest trees to gather firewood. There was no wind. The forest was silent. The snow continued to fall in a dream.

Keeping to the bracken to disguise her tracks, Ylva collected an armful of good sticks. After she had piled them at the base of the path up to the caves, she foraged a little deeper among the trees to find more. She needed enough to last until daylight.

The sound of wolves was still fresh in her mind, so

she moved slowly and in near silence, but as she strayed further from the cave, she heard something else; something out of place.

Ylva dropped the bundle of sticks and hurried to a shadowy patch of dense bracken, where she got down on her knees. She closed her eyes and listened to the skiff and thump of horses moving through the snow.

'We haven't seen hide nor hair of them since we reached the river,' a voice said. 'Where did they go?'

'All this snow isn't helping. As soon as a track is laid down, it's covered right up again.'

'Shh. Keep your voices down.'

Ylva gripped her makeshift spear and scooted on to her belly. She let the snow begin to bury her.

'We're not giving up.' This voice was muffled, but deep, like the rumble of wagon wheels. Ylva knew immediately who it was. 'Don't anybody suggest we give up.'

The three-fingered man came into view. Dressed head to toe in fur, he was a nightmare sitting atop his horse; a wolf-warrior riding into the world of the dead. The trees were dark skeletons against the stark whiteness of the snow, and the huge silhouette passed wraith-like among them. The horse wore thick leather armour to protect its head. Curved tusks protruded from either side of its muzzle, and it breathed out steam with each blustering breath. It was as if a fire burnt deep inside it.

Behind it, four other fur-clad riders emerged from the forest, moving in single file. They were no more than twenty paces from where Ylva was lying.

'We're chasing our tails out here.' A woman's voice

this time. The one who had stolen Mother's locket.

'They're here somewhere.' The three-fingered man spoke again. To Ylva's ears, it was the voice of a demon. Deep and smooth, and softer than it ought to be.

'We haven't seen anything since the river. We could be looking in the wrong place.'

'No. They're here.' The three-fingered man steadied his stallion and turned his head this way and that as he rode by.

Ylva held her breath; afraid he would catch her scent. She gripped the spear in her fist and felt such deep anger that she wanted to leap from the shadows and scream her battle cry as she had screamed at the bear. She had fought that beast, so why not this one? She could take her spear and run at the three-fingered man, driving the fire-hardened point into his chest. Bron's arrows had killed these warriors, so why not her spear?

'We'll split up.' As he spoke, the three-fingered man turned in Ylva's direction, and she was looking at a monster. 'We'll find them.' He wore a thick leather helmet with a nosepiece, and holes cut into the shape of wolf's eyes for him to see. Another piece of leather was fixed around the lower half of his face, covering his mouth, with the half-skull design painted on to it.

Now was the time.

Finish this. Kill him and be done.

But she didn't move. She couldn't do it alone. All she could do was watch the three-fingered man pass in front of her, moving between the trees, and vanish into the darkness.

29

Geri and Freki

———➤

'I saw him,' Ylva whispered when she was back at Cathryn's side. 'I went for firewood and saw the three-fingered man. He was right there in the woods. Him and four others. He's still looking for us.' She poked a stick at what was left of the fire. 'I think it's best to leave this for now. In case they come back.'

Cathryn opened her eyes and watched Ylva.

'I had my spear. He was right there. I could've killed him. I'm sure I could've. If only I'd . . . Ugh!' Ylva threw the stick aside in anger. 'I failed Mother. I should've avenged her right then.'

'Five warriors,' Cathryn said. 'If you'd attacked, you would've got yourself killed.'

'But I could've got him. If I died it wouldn't matter. I don't care about me.' She brought the wolf pup to her and held him in her lap.

'I don't believe that. I believe you're a survivor, child, that's why you're still here.' Cathryn shivered. 'You didn't attack him because you wouldn't have survived, and that wouldn't do, would it? For him to live and you to die?'

Ylva stared into the fire. 'It wouldn't be right.'

'Uh-huh. Or maybe it's something else altogether, Ylva the Fearless. You're letting the fire die, so you must be afraid he'll come back.'

'Afraid? I'm not afraid, I'm—'

'Concerned. I know.' Cathryn turned her head to face the ceiling of the cave. 'Did you hear the wolves?'

'I did.' Ylva took a strip of dried fish from the bag and offered it to Cathryn.

Cathryn glanced at it and shook her head. Ylva didn't feel like she could stomach anything, either, but she knew it was important to feed herself. She took a bite and forced herself to chew.

'And you know it's not him howling, don't you?' Cathryn said. 'That he can't turn into a wolf, and he isn't possessed by a wolf spirit.'

Ylva swallowed as a thought occurred to her. 'But if the three-fingered man is Ulfhednar, then maybe the wolves are helping him.'

'Child, I've been to many places and seen many things, but nothing has ever convinced me that magic is real. And even if Ulfhednar are real, the half-skulls are not them. I've already told you; they're just men, and Bron's arrows killed them dead enough. Remember that whenever you have any doubts.'

'Do you promise?'

'Yes.'

Ylva looked to the mouth of the cave and into the darkness of the forest. 'How far to Seatun?'

'A few hours' ride.' Cathryn closed her eyes.

'Then we should leave as soon as it's light.' Ylva tore off a piece of fish with her teeth and offered it to the pup. He sniffed it then tugged it from her fingers and swallowed it in one gulp. 'You're hungry.' She gave him another piece, and when he'd finished, she put her hand on the soft fur between his ears. The pup waited for more food, trying to lick her hand, but when it didn't come, he sniffed and buried his muzzle under her arm. Ylva lifted him up and put her face against the side of his head. His smell wasn't exactly like Geri's, but it was similar enough to bring a flood of memories. 'Do you think she's going to be all right?' she whispered in the pup's ear.

'I'm stabbed, not deaf.' Cathryn half opened her eyes. A smile broke her lips and she started to chuckle. It was a low, throaty sound.

'What's funny?' Ylva asked.

'Chased all over Midgard by a horde of half-skulls and I fall on my own knife.'

'That's not funny.'

'If I didn't laugh, child, I'd cry. And you know what else is funny? You and that pup. I think you just about deserve each other.'

'What does that mean?'

'It means each of you is as sorry-looking as the other. Wild and alone and halfway to being fierce.'

'I'm not alone; you're here. And I have the pup.' Ylva put him in her lap and held him there despite his complaints. 'I'll call him Freki,' she said. 'Odin has two wolves, Geri and Freki.'

'I know. And I understand why you want to keep him, but your dog was not a wolf, and that pup is not his brother. It's a wild animal and it will never be yours. It won't replace Geri.'

'No.' Ylva allowed Freki to wriggle free and run to the end of his leash. 'Nothing could ever replace Geri.'

'And he doesn't deserve to be collared like a slave.'

'He's not a slave,' Ylva said. 'He's my friend.'

'Perhaps you should let him decide that.'

30

Don't Look Back

Cathryn slept through most of the day, fever slowly consuming her. She mumbled in her troubled sleep, and her body shook as if spirits were fighting over it.

From time to time Ylva walked to the cave entrance and looked across the forest, knowing that the three-fingered man was out there somewhere. Relighting the fire was a risk, but the longer she waited, the more they needed warmth. Cathryn especially. Ylva put it off as long as she dared, hoping that Cathryn would improve and that they could leave for Seatun, but the woman's condition only worsened. Growing more afraid for Cathryn than she was of what might lie hidden among the trees, Ylva finally rekindled the fire and kept the flames burning low. What little smoke there was rose to the cave roof and dispersed before drifting out through the entrance. There was hardly any trace of it in the grey light of day.

As the cave warmed, Ylva checked Cathryn was still breathing. She lifted the woman's blanket and pulled up the hem of her tunic. When she untied the bandage and looked at the injury, she didn't like what she saw. The blood had stopped but the area around the wound was angry.

'This is bad.'

The wolf pup, Freki, lifted his head and pricked up his ears at the sound of her voice.

'Yes,' Ylva told him. 'It's very bad.'

Freki sniffed the air, then rested his head on his front paws and watched her, eyebrows twitching.

'Ylva.' Cathryn reached for Ylva's hand, taking her by surprise. 'There's nothing . . .' Cathryn took a moment to catch her breath, 'nothing you can do for me now. Go to Seatun and find Bron. He'll take you somewhere safe.'

'Without you?'

'This isn't getting better, Ylva. I'm dying. I feel it.'

'No.' Ylva shook her head and pulled away from her. 'I won't leave you.'

'There's no use you waiting here to watch me die.' Cathryn closed her eyes again. She was quiet for so long Ylva thought she'd fallen asleep. 'Get to Seatun. Find Bron. He'll keep you safe.'

'I can't go there on my own. A Dane in a Saxon village? They'll—'

'I told you; there's no one in Seatun to hurt you. You'll be safe there.'

'Then we'll go there together. You can sleep longer – another night – and we'll ride out in the morning.'

'You're not listening.'

'You helped me so I'm going to help you.'

'I'm not going anywhere. I can't walk. I can't ride.'

'I can build a sled and the horse can pull you.'

Cathryn tried to smile. 'There you go again, refusing to change your mind.'

'It shows strong character.'

'It's called being stubborn. Like a goat. Didn't your mother tell you that?'

'Yes.'

'She was a smart woman.'

'I'll build a sled,' Ylva said, as if it was the last word she was going to say about it.

'Things aren't always as they seem, Ylva. They don't always turn out how we want them to. Wanting something, really wanting it hard, doesn't make it happen, so don't waste any more time here. Get to Seatun. Find Bron. Tell him who you really are.' She reached up and touched Ylva's scarf. 'There's a lot of bad in this world, child, but you're the toughest person I ever met; you'll survive. I know you will.'

Ylva watched her.

'Take the horse. Ride north.' She let her hand drop. 'Seatun is in the first valley you come to. You'll see it. Bron will be waiting for you. Don't look back, She Wolf. Don't look back.'

They were the last words Cathryn spoke.

31

Night Terror

Ylva did head north, just like Cathryn told her, but not straight away. She didn't leave Cathryn to die alone.

She fed the fire through the cold, grim day, wood snapping and popping in the flames. She kept Cathryn warm and comfortable. When it was safe, she took the horse down to the forest to find a place for it to graze, but there was nothing for it to eat.

When darkness fell, the howling returned.

Ylva remembered what Cathryn had said: '*They're just men, and Bron's arrows killed them dead enough.*' Cathryn hadn't convinced her that Ulfhednar did not exist, but Ylva was starting to believe that the half-skulls were not possessed by wolf spirits. She told herself that although the man who killed Mother wore wolf furs on his back and a half-skull on his face, he was still just a man. He would be sleeping, eating, searching maybe, but he wasn't out there, howling in the forest.

The ground-tied horse moved restlessly in the cave entrance, and Ylva went to him. He put his head over her shoulder and she circled her arm around him. 'I know,' she said. 'You're afraid. Cold and tired and hungry. Just be strong for a while longer. When we get to Seatun, I'll give you all the feed I can find. Just be strong.'

The horse snorted and blew. He pulled his head away and moved from side to side, his ears turning.

Freki was uneasy too. He stood alert with every wild howl from the forest, but was afraid to venture close to the front of the cave.

'Easy.' Ylva soothed the horse, running the flat of her hand along his muscular neck. 'Easy.' She looked past him, into the night and down through the naked claws of the alders and birches below. Dark spirits moved against the stark white of the snow. Too small and lithe to be men on horseback, the silhouettes slipped among the trees like the blurred shapes of fish beneath water. In and out of view, they crept closer to the rocks, where they waited like hungry shadows.

Wolves.

Ylva took the horse deeper into the cave to try to settle him, but when the howls came again, they were loud and close, and he reared in blind terror. He turned on the spot, and Ylva held tight to his reins, but he was too strong. He bolted, yanking Ylva off her feet and dragging her across the rocks as he headed for the precipice at the cave entrance. If Ylva held on any longer, she would be dragged to her death, so there was nothing for her to do but let go.

Ylva released the reins and watched, waiting helplessly for the horse to go over the edge and disappear from view, but at the last moment, he turned. As if he had seen it just in time, his hooves clattered and he skidded to his right, following the ledge that led down to the snow. Ylva scrambled to her feet to go after him, but stopped when she saw wolves halfway along the ledge. Not men, not wolf-warriors, but wolves.

Three of them.

While the animals circling below had distracted her, others had been making their way up to the cave. They had been closing in on her, but now they scattered in surprise as the horse raced towards them. He slammed into the first one, knocking it off the ledge with a high-pitched yelp. The others leapt aside, and gathered themselves, but as soon as the horse had passed, they turned and gave chase.

Ylva hurried back into the cave and grabbed the spear, but when she returned to the ledge, the wolves and the horse were gone, and the night was quiet once more.

Alone

32

Nobody

Cathryn died before first light.

Ylva arranged her with weapons in her hands, then buried her beneath a mound of rocks collected from the cave floor.

Afterwards, she sat by the fire with the wolf pup curled in her lap.

'I lied,' she whispered to the mound of rocks. 'Mother wasn't a famous healer. My father wasn't a brave warrior. I'm nobody. I don't even know my father's name.'

An almost overwhelming sadness filled her heart, but Ylva dug her fingernails into the back of her hand and bit her lip. 'No,' she said. 'This is not the time for tears.'

When the sun rose, Ylva hung the goatskin bags across her shoulders. She tucked Freki into her cloak, picked up her spear, and took one last look at the mound of black stones in the centre of the cave.

'Goodbye,' she said, and set off into the forest once more.

>>———————>

North, Cathryn had told her. To the first valley she came to. That's where she would find Seatun.

She made slow progress on foot. Pushing through the understorey in the dense forest, the snow was manageable, but when the trees opened out, the covering was deep and difficult to navigate. In those places Ylva moved slowly, prodding the ground with her spear before each step.

She didn't think about Mother. She didn't think about Geri, or Cathryn. She didn't want any distractions at all so she thought of nothing other than putting one foot in front of the other and heading north. Just north.

The cold was harsh, but the air was still. There was no wind for her to fight, and Ylva was thankful for the clear morning that let her see the sun. Without it, she wouldn't have known north from south.

As the afternoon wore on, Ylva began to feel that she would never leave the forest. Only when she was beginning to lose hope did she notice a familiar scent carried on the breeze. And when she finally emerged from the trees, she stopped on a rocky plateau that overlooked the valley Cathryn had told her about. Far below, the whole valley floor was the purest white. It was as if clouds had fallen from the sky, and had been rippled into gentle waves by the winter winds. At the far end of the valley the forest climbed the distant hills, but to her right, the glittering sea crashed on a sandy beach, and Ylva breathed deeply, tasting the salty air that reminded her of home.

But more recent memories – uglier memories – washed over those happy thoughts of a Viking village by the sea. It was difficult to look at that English beach and not think of the burning ship she and Mother had fled. Of screams in the surf and blood in the sand.

Hair blowing around her face, she watched the breakers rolling in from the misty sea, wondering why the gods had let this happen to her. Why had they led her here? She turned her attention to what lay in the middle of the valley, close to the water.

Seatun.

Was this where the gods wanted her to come?

The sun was inching lower over the valley, spilling a blazing orange glow that seared across the snow and shimmered on the sea. Into that white world aflame, the town of Seatun settled like a seed of hope. Ylva counted no more than thirty thatched wooden buildings arranged in no particular order, with a tall wooden wall to surround and protect them. There were pens and barns for keeping animals. Ylva could already feel the closeness of civilization. But the longer she watched, the more she sensed there was something not quite right about Seatun.

She saw no movement. No people. No animals. She stared until her eyes watered from the strain, and decided the lack of movement was because of the cold. Everyone must be inside, keeping warm. That was the only answer.

So why is there no smoke? Why is there not a single fire burning in Seatun? Why are the roofs still heavy with snow?

As she stood and wondered, there was a clatter of wings from a pair of ravens flying out of the forest behind her.

Raak! Raak! they protested as they soared over the valley like Huginn and Munnin, the two great ravens that carried news to Odin.

Ylva turned slowly to scan the trees behind her. From the warmth and safety of her cloak, Freki watched too. Just his head was visible, and Ylva felt the soft tips of his ears under her chin as they pricked up, swivelling to find any sound.

'Something disturbed them,' she whispered as she cast her gaze over the trees. 'Do you see anything?' But the longer she watched, the less she saw, and when she looked back at the village in the valley below, Ylva wanted to be there. When they reached it, she would find warmth and hot food, and she would begin her search for someone who would help her fulfil her promise to Mother.

And once she was ready, she would find the three-fingered man, she would kill him, and the gods would stop punishing her.

>>>—→

Ylva held tight to the warm bundle beneath her cloak and stretched the awkwardness from her muscles. She moved to the edge of the plateau and looked down the steep climb. 'I don't like this,' she whispered to Freki. 'I don't like this at all.'

The first part of the climb was gentle. Ylva stepped

sideways to avoid slipping, and planted her feet firmly with each step. One wrong move and the snow would tumble away from beneath her and she would fall.

'Slow and steady,' she told Freki as she held tight to him with one hand. With the other, she clung to the puny saplings that grew in the thin soil between the rocks.

The goatskin bags grew heavy across her shoulders, and carrying the pup made everything more awkward, so by the time she was halfway down the valley wall, the sun was low in the west. If she didn't pick up her pace, it would be dark long before she made it to Seatun. But there was no way she could move any faster; she had reached the place where the descent became much harder. From here, the valley wall was steeper, and there were places where the drop was sheer, straight down to the seashore below. Ylva scanned ahead, searching for the easiest route, and as she stood on the ledge, trying to find a way down, a wolf began to howl in the forest above.

Freki squirmed inside her cloak.

'Hush now.' Ylva squeezed him tighter. 'You'll make me fall. It isn't much further, I just need to find the right route and we'll be fine.'

The deadly effect of Bron's arrows, combined with Cathryn's insistence, had convinced Ylva that the three-fingered man was not Ulfhednar. And seeing the wolves last night had shown her that it hadn't been the half-skulls howling in the forest. But now Ylva understood that the half-skulls were not the only predators hunting her. Hungry wolves had found her scent, too. They had taken her horse, and now they wanted her.

The wolf howled again and Ylva turned to look up at the way she had come. It was a mistake. The whiteness of the snow, the patches of black rock, and the passing of the clouds made her head spin. And when the pup wriggled inside her cloak, Ylva lost her balance. She felt herself tip backwards. The sky moved, the mountainside slipped away, and Ylva dropped like she would fall for ever.

33

Hunted

Ylva hit rock with a sudden and dreadful thump. She landed on her back, and bounced, slipping further down the cliff. The snow was deep, but it hardly cushioned her at all. Ylva felt every hard edge as she skidded and spun backwards towards the valley floor. But she didn't put out her hands to snatch at the saplings to stop her fall. Instead, she wrapped her arms tight around herself to protect the pup that nestled inside her cloak. She kept him safe until she slammed into a large outcrop and came to a bone-crunching stop. Her head whipped back and cracked against the hard surface, and everything went dark.

When she opened her eyes again, it felt as if hours had passed, but it couldn't have been more than a few seconds. A minute at the most. From her position, lying on her back propped against the outcrop that had stopped her, Ylva saw clear evidence of where she had fallen – a messy path straight down the mountainside. Far above was the black lip of the plateau, and beyond that the blue sky with the passing clouds.

Hurting all over, Ylva gave herself a minute to collect her thoughts. Freki wriggled free of her cloak, poking his head out. He whined and licked at the fresh blood on the scrapes across her chin. She pushed him away and checked he was still in one piece.

'Looks like you came out of that better than I did.'

She set him down beside her and sat up, realizing for the first time that the goatskin bags were gone. There was no sign of them anywhere near her, so she crouched behind the outcrop, wiped the blood from her chin, and looked up to see if she could spot them. That's when she caught sight of movement at the edge of the plateau high above her.

At first she thought of the three-fingered man. But when she brushed her hair out of her eyes and squinted against the brightness of the snow and the sky, she saw something different.

A large black wolf was looking down at her.

➤➤➤──────→

With its dark snout and its pointed ears silhouetted against the light, it could almost have been Geri standing up there on the ridge watching her. But Geri was dead, and the shape above was not a figment of Ylva's imagination. The black wolf was real, and Ylva needed to get away from it, so she gathered herself and came down into the bay as quickly as she could. She sat on her backside and slid most of the way, using the rocks and saplings to guide her. She wished she had thought of doing it earlier, but it was too late for that now. Decisions never were her strong point, and there was no good to be had from wishing she had done this or that. Wishing was for fools. The only way anything ever got done was by rolling up your sleeves and doing it, not by wishing for it. That's what Mother always said, and Ylva was sure Cathryn would have agreed with her.

Behind her, the wolf howled again, and this time the call was answered by another howl. Then another, and another, until the wolves drowned out the sound of her sliding in the snow. The howling was all she could hear. High and tuneful. Beautiful and terrifying. With their howls echoing from the trees behind her, Ylva believed the forest could be full of wolves. They were calling to each other, bringing the pack together, and then they would hunt.

When she reached the bottom, Ylva clutched Freki to her chest and got to her feet. The perfect snow was so deep it came to her knees.

She looked back at the wide trail leading down from the plateau. At the very top of it, four wolves had left the cover of the trees and stood on the ridge, snapping and yelping as they agitated each other. Ylva thought they might stay where they were, unwilling to leave the safety of the forest, but it wasn't long before three more wolves joined the pack, and the animals began their descent.

Ylva watched them pick their way down, following the same path she had taken, and she knew they would move faster than she could.

Aching from the bruises already forming on her back and shoulders, she pulled her cloak tight around her, drew the axe from her belt, and hurried closer to the sea. She didn't want to get her feet wet, but there was no snow where the water touched the sand, so it was easier for her to pick up her pace and jog towards the distant town, boots splashing in the surf.

The wolves hung back, pausing their descent every few minutes to tease and agitate one another. The sound of their yips and yowls blended with the crashing of the breakers on the beach. Even when they reached the valley floor, they kept their distance. They followed the same route Ylva had taken, but from time to time several of them would break away from the main group to scout into the deep snow further inland.

Some were black, gliding like shadows. Others were grey, or close to white, and it was difficult to keep track of them. Sometimes Ylva counted seven shapes running together, nipping at each other, and other times she saw only three or four.

She wondered what they were doing; perhaps they were wondering about her too. Maybe they were deciding if she were suitable prey. Maybe they would give up.

But the wolves didn't give up. The pack followed her across the bay as if they would never tire, so Ylva kept moving towards the village in the distance.

The sun was dazzling and the cold was punishing. Ylva's hands were stiff and painful, and she had lost the feeling in her face. There were times she felt as if she were stuck in one spot. When she looked behind, the mountains and the forest seemed no further away, and when she looked ahead, Seatun was no closer. It was as if she were in a dream, running hard, but never going anywhere.

As the afternoon wore on, and the sun dropped, Ylva knew the gods were conspiring against her, because the sky darkened first to a dirty grey, and then to a sombre black. The wind picked up, heavy thunderheads rolled over the distant hills, and Thor began to beat his hammer.

As the world fell into a grey gloom and more snow began to fall, Ylva continued on. She didn't stop before she reached Seatun. But the wind was fierce and the snow was blinding, and when she looked back, the wolves were lost in the storm.

34

Ghosts in the Storm

➤➤➤➤➤⟶

The sea faded, and the valley filled with swirling flakes of snow that danced in the ever-changing wind.

Unable to see more than a short distance in front of her, Ylva pressed on and on. She kept close to the shore, afraid she would lose her way and end up walking in circles. She didn't even look back, searching for the wolves. There was nothing she could do about them. All she could do was keep moving.

When she thought she was nearing the village, she veered away from the sea, heading further inland. For a while she wondered if it had been a mistake to lose the beach as a point of reference, but finally a dark shape appeared out of the storm like a ghost ship from a misty sea. Coming closer, she made out what she guessed was the village wall, and felt a sudden and overwhelming sense of relief. Safety was within reach; a place to be warm and comfortable.

But Ylva's relief began to slip away when she passed an ancient, decaying cart. And when she entered the open village gates, she saw that the deep snow along the paths between the huts was untouched. To her left, one side of the town was just a silhouette in the storm, but to her right, it was evident where the weather had taken its toll on the wooden buildings, and no one had made any attempt to repair them. Every inch of ground was thick with snow. Roofs were broken, shutters were cracked, wooden walls were rotten away. It dawned on her that this was not an occupied village.

Seatun was abandoned.

'Why didn't you tell me?' She spoke to the wind as her heart sank. 'You let me think there were people here.' She turned on the spot, frustration building. An overwhelming sense of hopelessness settled in her hollow stomach. She had come so far. Survived so much. She had struggled to this place with the promise of hope flickering inside her. But now she saw the truth of Seatun.

'There's no one here. There hasn't been anyone here for years.' She turned her face to the sky. 'Why didn't you tell me? You let me think . . .' But she was too frustrated to speak. Her throat was constricted. She clenched her jaw and squeezed her eyes shut. Seatun wasn't a safe haven. Seatun wasn't a place to find help or hope. Seatun was just a convenient place to meet; a forgotten place where no one would ever think to search for her. And when she stared out towards the sea, with the wind in her face, she knew what must have happened to Seatun.

The bay was a perfect place for Viking raiders to draw their boats ashore. They would have taken everything, and killed everyone.

➤

When she had composed herself, Ylva turned to look back the way she had come, as if she could look through the storm, the mountains, the trees, all the way to where Cathryn lay beneath a mound of stones in Barghest Caves.

'Why didn't you tell me? You could've told me.'

Freezing cold, standing in the middle of an abandoned town, Ylva's disappointment and despair threatened to overcome her. She was tempted to sit down in the snow and let nature take her.

No. You still have to keep your promise to Mother. You have to stay alive. There's no other option. You have to avenge us.

Thinking the words, imagining Geri using them, Ylva longed for him to be with her. Every fibre in her body ached to see him, to hold him again. He always kept her strong when she needed him. And as she stood gathering her resolve, making herself strong, Ylva realized she was not alone in Seatun.

A dark and ghostly shape was moving close by, blurred by the storm.

As soon as she saw it, everything was forgotten. All that mattered now was the shape; a shape that was too tall to be a wolf.

Freki squirmed, trying to escape, but Ylva ignored him. She kept her eyes on the blurred silhouette and raised her axe, coiling herself ready to strike as the figure loomed closer. Lean and dark, almost indistinguishable beneath his cloak, the boy stopped no more than a few paces away from her.

'It's you.' Ylva kept her axe ready but stayed where she was.

Bron held a bow in his hands. The supple wood was curved, the string was pulled back, and an arrow was aimed directly at Ylva's heart.

'Point that thing somewhere else.' Ylva lowered her weapon. 'We need to get inside. There are wolves following me.'

The boy stared at her for a long while, then shifted his eyes to glance into the storm.

'Cathryn's gone,' Ylva said. 'She fell on her knife and . . .' She dropped her arm. 'She's gone.'

Bron kept the bow pointed at Ylva. It was as if the storm had frozen him solid right where he stood.

'We have to get inside,' Ylva said again.

Bron grunted once, then lowered the bow and moved past her, heading deeper into Seatun. Ylva followed a few paces behind, walking among the houses towards a pair of larger buildings that were set back from the others.

>>>———————>

The boy led Ylva to the smith's workshop and went inside. The dim, dark room had a bare dirt floor and smelt like wood and dust and fire. A small amount of grey light filtered through the shutters on either side at the back – just enough for Ylva to see that whoever worked here had left all their belongings behind.

Horseshoes hung from nails hammered into the roof beams, criss-crossed with cobwebs that fluttered in the draught. A worktable was strewn with blackened, dust-laden tools. More hung from hooks, creaking as they swung in the wind that fingered through the cracks in the walls. A pair of old saddles lay slumped in one corner like dead beasts. Beside them was a collection of barrels – some cut in half and full of stagnant water.

There was a crude bed of straw and fur close to the stone forge in the centre of the back wall, suggesting that Bron had been here a while already.

'We need a fire.' Ylva approached the forge. 'I'll make one in here.'

The boy shook his head. He touched two fingers to his eyes and pointed them away towards the wall.

'You think someone will see?'

Bron nodded.

'No one can see anything in this storm, and we need a fire or we'll freeze to death.' There were still remnants of charred wood and ash in the furnace, but they were cold and long dead. Beside it, the supply of wood and charcoal was dusty and strung with cobwebs.

Ylva put Freki down to let him investigate the room as she built the fire. She used a splash of lamp oil she found in a barrel, and within minutes the wood was roaring. She fed it with charcoal to help it burn hotter, and busied herself lighting some of the lamps she found hanging from nails on the pillars that supported the roof. As she waited for the warmth to fill the room, she sat on the stone forge surround, wrapped her arms around herself, and watched Freki sniffing about the room.

Bron sat on the opposite side of the forge, but Ylva couldn't bring herself to look at him.

'I tried to stop the bleeding, but she had a fever,' she said after a while.

Pain contorted the boy's face as he forced a whispered word from his lips. 'Where?'

It took Ylva by surprise. She hadn't expected him to speak. 'Barghest Caves. I buried her there.'

Bron stood up. He turned and made for the door.

'Wait,' Ylva called after him. 'Where are you going?'

Bron ignored her and pulled the door open. As soon as he did, the wind blasted into the workshop, bringing the snow with it.

'What are you going to do?' Ylva secured Freki's leash to stop him from escaping the workshop, then went after Bron. She moved slowly. Her whole body was aching and stiff from her fall to the valley floor, so Bron was already in the stable next door when she caught up with him. His chestnut horse was in one of the stalls, and he was about to lift a saddle over its back, so Ylva grabbed his cloak and pulled him hard.

Bron dropped the saddle and glared at her. He pointed a thumb at his chest then at the horse before pointing outside.

'You're going to take the horse out in this storm?'

He nodded.

'You want to go to the cave? Is that where you're going? To do what? It's half a day's ride in good weather, but now? With a horse that's tired and hungry? It's too far. And there are wolves out there. A whole pack of them.'

Bron stooped to pick up the saddle, so Ylva grabbed his cloak again. 'You'll never make it,' she said.

The boy pulled against her.

'I won't let you.'

Bron shoved Ylva hard, trying to push her away, but she held on to his cloak and they both went down into the stale straw. Bron fell on top of her, his full weight pushing her down so that Ylva couldn't breathe. Her face was smothered by Bron's cloak and she struggled beneath him, freeing her arms and reaching up to beat at his back, scratch at the side of his head. She kicked her feet and brought her knees up to hurt him. 'I won't let you!' she shouted. 'I won't let you leave me!'

Bron pushed away from her, fighting off her flailing attack. He fell sideways and Ylva took advantage of the moment, spinning around and climbing on top of him. She sat astride his chest, and raised her fists to hit him, but before she could land a single blow, Bron reached up and put the blade of his knife against her throat.

Ylva stopped.

She looked down into the boy's eyes. 'You want to kill me? Then do it. Kill me and let this all be finished. Make it all go away.'

But Ylva's cloak had loosened during their struggle. Bron had pulled her scarf away, and now his expression softened as he stared at what she had been hiding beneath the wool.

A narrow ring of crude, black iron was fastened around her neck. A slave collar that rubbed her skin raw.

As soon as Ylva understood that he had seen it, she looked away.

Bron lowered the knife and let his hand fall to the floor.

35

Friend

Ylva and Bron kept to opposite sides of the workshop, as if a great sea flowed between them. Bron stayed by his bed, close to the furnace, while Ylva rested her aching back against a tree stump with a battered anvil on top of it.

Bron knew she was a slave – that she was wearing an iron collar – but she had adjusted the scarf to cover it anyway. She didn't want him to look at it.

The pup bustled about the room with his nose to the ground, pleased not to be squashed inside Ylva's cloak any more. He sniffed every corner, investigated every shadow, then went around to check them all again. Finally, he settled beneath the worktable, close to where Ylva was sitting.

The longer Ylva looked at him, the more he faded

into the gloom. His black fur camouflaged him in the darkness beneath the table, and unless Ylva blinked, he began to look like nothing more than a dark blur staring out at her with mismatched eyes.

'Cathryn wanted me to kill him and leave him with his dead mother.' Ylva didn't look at Bron when she spoke to him. 'She understood why I didn't, though. She saw why.'

Ylva extended her hand towards the pup. 'It's not just because they killed my dog. It's not that. I know Freki can't replace him. It's because, in a way, he's like me, and . . . and Cathryn said we deserved each other. She said it was because we're both as wild as each other. Even with a collar. But I'm no wilder than you, Bron. Probably not even *as* wild as you. So he's like you too.'

The pup sniffed the air and inched forward, bringing his nose closer. He stayed that way for a moment, then shoved his nose into Ylva's hand and put out his tongue to lick her palm.

'She told me to leave her.' Ylva looked over at Bron and their eyes met. 'In the caves. We stopped there for two nights and I cleaned the wound, put some moss on it, but I couldn't stop the fever. That's when she said I should leave her, but I couldn't, so I stayed with her until she was gone.' Ylva chewed the inside of her cheek. 'I think she was a good person. I liked her.'

Bron sighed. There was a deep change in his expression, and when he looked away, Ylva lowered her eyes to the pup and ran her hand over his head.

On the opposite side of the workshop, Bron got to his feet. He came to stand in front of Ylva and look down at her sitting against the tree stump. He paused, then turned to the table and rummaged through the dusty tools, sending spiders scuttling for cover. When he found what he was looking for, he crouched in front of Ylva and reached out to move her scarf. Ylva put up her hands to resist, so Bron stopped and showed her what he had taken from the table.

Understanding what he was going to do, Ylva allowed him to remove the scarf, and she watched his eyes as he lifted the metal shears and cut through the fastening at the front of her collar. It took all his strength, but when it was done, he placed the shears on the floor beside him and took the collar from around Ylva's neck. He held it out for her to take.

'They didn't always make us wear them.' She let it hang open in her fingers. 'Our owner wasn't even all that bad. Much better than some of the others. I played with his children, ate with his family. He never beat or sacrificed his slaves, but no one should own another person, should they? And even when I wasn't wearing this –' she threw the collar to one side – 'I still had this.' Ylva pulled the neck of her tunic across to show Bron the blue mark tattooed on the front of her left shoulder.

'Mother told me it means "fehu",' she said. 'Cattle. My owner put it there when I was born. To show I was his property.'

Bron put the scarf back around Ylva's neck and pulled

her cloak tight. He gave her a sad smile and put the index finger of each hand together as if they were hooking one another.

'Friend,' he said.

><<---->

When Bron sat down in front of her, Ylva asked him, 'Did you already know? About that?' She looked at the iron collar lying on the floor.

Bron nodded. He put both hands on the right side of his face, palms open, and tilted his head.

'You saw it when I was sleeping? In the trader's hut? So you always knew?'

He nodded again.

'I didn't want anyone to know. Mother said it was dangerous. Runaway slaves get beaten. People do horrible things to them and . . .' She put a hand into her hair and tugged on it. She couldn't believe they had known all this time. It made her feel foolish. But there was also a sense of weight lifting from her shoulders. At least for now, she didn't need to lie any more. Not to Bron, anyway. She had nothing to hide from him now, and nothing to fear from him. He was her friend.

'Why did you come to England?' His voice was quiet and hoarse.

'Our owner said this place belonged to the Danes now.' Ylva took her hand from her hair and put it to her neck, where the skin was free from the iron collar. 'Someone told him there was good farmland, but he shouldn't have crossed the sea in winter. Not when the waves are bigger than mountains. We were blown off course, and when we landed, we were attacked before we even escaped the beach. Saxons murdered everyone. I suppose they must hate Vikings.' She closed her eyes at the memory of it. Slaves she had known all her life were killed that day. Her owner, too, his wife and children, other men and women from their village. None of them had deserved to die like that; not even her owner. 'The sea and the sand were red with blood,' she said. 'So much blood.'

Telling her story, saying the words out loud, was like rubbing ointment on a deep wound. It didn't heal the injury, but it softened the pain, and tears of grief threatened to come. But Ylva bit them back. This was not the time. Her tears would have to wait.

'Mother and I escaped into the forest with Geri, and when the Saxons were gone, we went back to take whatever they'd left, anything we could use, but there wasn't much more than a knife and a loaf of bread. And then we set off to find . . . I don't know. Something better.' She chewed her lips and looked through her hair at Bron. 'We didn't find anything better, though, did we? And now I'm like you. Alone.'

'No,' Bron whispered. 'We're not alone.'

36

The Call of the Wild

Outside, the wind picked up, blowing through the ghostly village. And in that emptiness, a single wolf howled once. It was not distant, as it had been in the forest; this sound was loud and close, and there was no doubt it had come from somewhere in the village.

The pup took to his feet in Ylva's lap. His ears pricked up and he stood stock-still. A quiet growl rumbled in his throat before he lost his courage and leapt down to disappear under the workbench. Ylva stayed where she was, hardly daring to breathe, but the village remained quiet. The only sound was the wind whistling through the cracks in the walls, and the gentle squeak and rattle of tools swinging from their fixings.

Bron looked up at her. He shaped two fingers into an

upward 'V', like the ears of an animal.

'Wolf,' Ylva said.

Bron nodded.

Ylva drew her axe and went to the door. She tested it was locked, then scanned the room to see if there were any places where the wolves might get in. 'They came last night,' she said. 'To the cave. They took my horse, and now they've followed me here. What do they want? Are they hungry?'

Bron made the sign for wolf again. Then he put his fingers to his mouth before pointing at Ylva and himself while shaking his head.

'Wolves don't eat people?' Ylva guessed. 'Is that what you're saying?'

He nodded.

'Well they want something. We have to check the walls.' Some of the wood was weather-worn and rotten right through, so Ylva lifted one of the lamps from its nail and made her way around the workshop, testing the boards. She held the light close to look for weak spots, and pushed her weight against each one in turn. 'Help me.'

Bron checked the door, just as Ylva had done. Then he took another lamp and began to test the walls, working his way around the room in the opposite direction.

When Ylva came to the window on the left side of the back wall, she secured the shutter before making her way past the forge towards the window on the other side.

She put her face close to cracks in the shutter and held the lamp high. She looked out into the swirling white of the snowstorm blowing through the silent village. 'I see something.'

Bron hung his lamp back on its nail and grabbed his bow. He drew an arrow from the quiver and came to Ylva's side in time to see a dark shape sweep past the window. He glanced at Ylva and pointed two fingers upwards, like ears.

Wolf.

Ylva pressed her face even closer to the shutter and turned her head, trying to see. Lamplight leaked out into the storm, creating a fuzzy arc of weak orange in which snow glittered and danced. And as she stared, two more shapes floated by in the storm.

'They can't get in,' she said. 'They can't—'

Another shape appeared, passing from right to left across her field of vision, but this one didn't disappear into the shadow beyond the reach of the lamplight. This one stopped.

A blurry shape hanging in the white-out. A shape that grew larger as the animal crept forward. It was as if the great wolf Fenrir had broken his chains at Ragnarök – the end of everything; the destruction of the nine worlds – and had come to devour his first victims. It moved with its head down, its jaws open, blazing amber eyes glaring up at the window. It was the same creature Ylva had seen looking down at her from the plateau after she had fallen. There was no mistaking it. This animal was bigger than any dog she had ever known; bigger even than the wolf she had seen battling with the bear. It moved slowly, powerful muscles rippling beneath its dark coat. The fur was lighter around its eyes and mouth as if it were wearing its war mask.

The enormous wolf raised the tip of its nose to bare its teeth.

'Leave us alone.' Ylva gripped the axe tight in her fist.

The beast stared at her.

'Leave us alone!'

The wolf planted its feet and shuffled its hindquarters as if it were preparing to strike. The only barrier between Ylva and the wolf was a thin shutter of rotten wood. Perhaps it would take just one strong leap for it to break into the workshop, and the world would be full of splintered wood, and teeth and claws.

'Leave us alone!' Ylva raised the axe and stepped back to stand beside Bron. She held her weapon ready to fight, and waited for the sound of breaking wood, but it didn't come. Instead, the wolf put back its head and howled.

It was loud; as if the beast was with them inside the workshop. High-pitched and terrifying, it was the most primal sound Ylva could imagine. The call of a hunter in the wild; a creature with the most perfect instinct for the kill. An animal that would never give up.

When it stopped, Ylva spoke into the eerie silence. 'What do they want? Why are they doing this?' She backed away and turned on the spot, wondering where was the safest place in the room. Only by the workbench would she be able to see the door and both windows, so she went to the bench and sat on the floor. With the axe in one hand, she picked up Freki with the other, holding him to her chest. 'Don't be scared,' she said to him. 'Don't be scared. They'll give up and go away. You'll see.'

The wolf howled again in the emptiness of Seatun, and the others joined its call, yipping and snarling at the night. Inside, Freki tilted his head to one side. He stiffened his front legs and pushed away from Ylva, turning his ears towards the sound. He listened for a moment, then did something that neither Ylva nor Bron expected; he turned his nose to the ceiling and did his best to howl.

Freki's first attempt came out like a whine, but he repeated his effort until he managed something close to a high-pitched howl. When he had done it, he looked proud of himself and pushed his muzzle into Ylva's neck.

Outside, the wolves fell quiet. Ylva looked at Bron and strained to hear any sound. She listened as Cathryn had taught her to listen. At first, there was nothing except the wind, but the harder she listened, the more she heard. The squeak of the tools swinging above her head. The steady in and out of Bron's breath. The wet sound as the pup licked its lips. A low growl. A shuffle and a sigh.

A soft rasp against the back wall. Another at the door. More sounds from all around the workshop.

Ylva opened her eyes and looked at Bron. 'They're everywhere,' she said. 'They're trying to get in.'

37

Ragnarök

———➤

Keeping the pup in her arms, Ylva got to her feet and moved to the centre of the workshop as she listened to the wolves circling the building. They didn't howl any more. Instead they sniffed. And scraped. And Ylva imagined the huge black wolf burying its nose in the snow at the base of the wall, searching for her scent. Searching for a way in.

'What do you want?' she shouted.

Bron stood beside her, an arrow in one hand, and his bow in the other. He turned on the spot, watching the walls.

Thump!

They both jumped as the door rattled in its frame.

Thump!

Ylva felt the impact shake the whole building. Dust

fell from the roof beams and glittered in the lamplight.

'Go away!' Ylva shouted. 'Leave us alone!'

Bron nudged her to attract her attention. He put a finger to his mouth and shook his head, making it clear he wanted her to be quiet.

'What are they doing?' Ylva whispered.

The boy clamped his jaw tight and looked at the pup in Ylva's arms.

Thump!

This time the sound came from the back of the workshop.

Thump!

At the side wall now.

'They're throwing themselves against the wood,' Ylva breathed. 'Looking for a way in.' And when the next thump was followed by a sharp crack, Ylva knew they had found one.

She spun around, axe raised towards the wall close to the window where she had looked out at the beasts. There was another thump, and a ripping sound as one of the boards split. It splintered inwards, and another hard thump snapped it completely, throwing the broken piece of wood into the workshop. It skidded across the straw-scattered dirt floor and stopped close to where Ylva and Bron were standing.

They looked down at the chunk of smashed wood, then up at the gap in the wall. It was no wider than Ylva's hand, no longer than her arm, but they knew it was the start of something bigger.

A black muzzle pressed through, sniffing the air inside the workshop.

'Go away!' Ylva shouted.

The wolf turned its head sideways to look into the room. Ylva saw only one of its golden eyes.

Bron lifted his bow and pulled back the string, but as he released his hold and let the arrow fly, the wolf withdrew. As if it had known what he was doing. The arrow sailed across the workshop and disappeared through the gap in the boards. It didn't even touch the sides.

Immediately, the wolf was back, teeth snapping at the splintered wood, tearing at it, trying to make it wider. Bron took another arrow, drew back his bowstring, and fired, but the wolf retreated once more.

And then the others were throwing themselves at the wall again. Over and over, so the workshop was a nightmare of thumping and splitting and growling.

Bron stood with his bow ready, but Ylva backed away from the gap in the wall. She held Freki tight to her chest and gripped the axe, glancing at Bron to see that he only had a few more arrows left in his quiver. Even if every shot hit its mark, he wouldn't have enough to kill every wolf. And Ylva was beginning to doubt that arrows would even stop them. They were too big. Too fast. Too clever.

'Don't waste your arrows,' she told him.

Bron stopped with his bow drawn and ready, aiming at the gap in the wall. The planks around it groaned and cracked under the continued assault. Soon they would split and the wolves would be inside. He hesitated and looked at Ylva, then at the pup in her arms. His eyes widened as if something that was bothering him had suddenly become clear. 'The pup.' He lowered his bow and grabbed Freki by the scruff of the neck.

'What are you doing?' Ylva kept tight hold of the young wolf, but Bron pulled harder.

'No!' Ylva shouted. 'I won't let you have him!' She kicked out, catching Bron in the shin, making him let go of the pup and stumble backwards.

At that moment, the wall finally gave in. With a loud crack, the planks split and the huge black wolf tumbled into the workshop in a flurry of teeth and fur. It crashed into Bron, knocking him to the floor, and sent his bow spinning across the workshop.

The wolf scrambled to its feet and whipped around to face them like Fenrir facing Thor at the end of the world, and in a fraction of a second, Ylva took everything in.

The wolf, with its head down, its teeth bared, and its eyes blazing. More wolves surging forward to enter the workshop through the broken wall. Bron lying on the floor, with his bow out of reach. And herself, with her axe in her hand, ready to battle a pack of wolves.

But she knew her axe would be no match for a whole pack of wild animals.

Without thinking, she stuffed the axe into her belt, snatched the oil lamp from the nail beside her, and threw it at the wolf.

The lamp spun end over end as it sailed across the workshop. It went over Bron's head and came down directly in front of the black wolf, hitting the ground with a crash, breaking open, and spilling oil into the straw. There wasn't much left in it, but some splattered on to the wolf's front paws and burst into flames.

The animal yelped in fear. It rose up as if it were going to walk on two legs, then jumped back, turning in a circle before hurrying out through the gap in the wall.

But Ylva knew that once the wolf was in the deep snow, the flames would be gone, and the beast would come back. She had to stop it. She had to stop them all. She was hardly even thinking as she hurried to the other lamps, hurling them one by one at the gap in the wood. She threw them in a frenzy, as hard as she could, smashing them against the wall, splattering oil in all directions. Most of it splashed across the rotten wood, catching light and burning in streaks. Some fell to the straw where it sprouted in miniature bonfires. But some of it hit close to the half-barrel of oil that Ylva had used to fill the lamps and light the fire.

Flames erupted around the barrel, devouring the fuel Ylva had spilt earlier. They snaked up the sides of the container, found their way inside, and the oil ignited in the blink of an eye. It flared up like a giant lamp; a blaze of orange and black rose from the open barrel. It reached up to the ceiling and spread outwards, the flames rolling over one another.

The heat was intense. Ylva felt it smother her as she stumbled backwards, raising her hand against it. Freki panicked and squirmed in her arms, desperate to break free and escape the nightmare of heat and light. But Ylva held him tight.

'Get up!' she shouted at Bron.

He was still on the floor, close to the barrel, but there was no time to get to his feet, so he pushed himself backwards in the dirt, snatching up his bow as he went. Fiery rain dripped from the ceiling, spattering over his furs. It ignited on his body, burning his arms, and within seconds, he was aflame and panicking.

Ylva ran forwards and grabbed the back of his collar with one hand. She planted her feet firmly and dragged him away from the worst of the fire. She let go of Freki, and rolled Bron over and over to smother the flames on his furs. When the worst of it was out, he jumped to his feet in panic, swatting at himself as if he were still burning. Smoke rose from blackened patches on his furs.

'We have to get out.' Ylva pulled him further away from the searing inferno and shoved him towards the front of the workshop.

Coming to his senses, Bron hurried to the door and threw off the drop-bar. Ylva went to the workbench and got down on her knees. She reached under and grabbed Freki by the scruff of his neck. She dragged him out, despite his protests, and hurried to meet Bron by the door.

As soon as he opened it, a surge of cold air blasted into the room. There was a great *whoosh!* as the fire fed on the fresh oxygen, and the inferno rolled across the ceiling like an ocean of flames drowning the workshop.

Ylva and Bron stumbled out into the snow and staggered towards the stable before they turned to watch the workshop burn. By now the entire building was engulfed. The heat was incredible. Orange light illuminated the blizzard, and the smell of oil and woodsmoke was thick in Ylva's nostrils.

'Look.' She pointed deeper into the abandoned

village, where the light from the fire reached far enough for them to see into the white flurry of the snowstorm. There, the dark shapes of the wolves slipped along the fronts of the decaying buildings. They ran in panic towards the village gates, and Ylva knew they would escape into the valley, terrified by the fire.

38

Hate

Embers rose into the blizzard like flickering fireflies in distant summer. If they came close to the stable, Ylva and Bron stamped them out, but there wasn't much else they could do but watch the workshop burn until eventually it collapsed in on itself. In those final moments, a plume of sparks and black smoke rose into the sky, and when the workshop was no more than a glowing pile of ash, Ylva and Bron stood side by side; exhausted, aching and hungry.

'I hate him.' Ylva held Freki close to her chest. 'The three-fingered man, I mean. This is all his fault.' She stared at the coals as they blushed in the breeze. 'And now we have to go. He'll have seen the flames from the other end of the valley. He'll come looking for us and ... Wait.' She stopped as a thought leapt into her head so suddenly it was as if Thor had put it there himself. 'I've done enough running. We should wait for him.' She turned to Bron. 'We'll find a place to hide, and when he comes, we'll ambush him. We'll kill him. You with your arrows and me with my axe.'

The boy circled his fist in front of his face and tapped his head.

'I'm not stupid,' Ylva said. 'And I know you think I can't fight, but I can. I'm strong. I *can* fight. I fought a *bear* to get here. Those wolves, too. And I just saved your life.'

Bron shrugged. *So what?*

'So I'm going to stay here and wait for the three-fingered man.' She pulled the axe from her belt. 'And when he gets here, I'm going to kill him, and all this will be over.'

'You want to kill me, child? I don't think so.' The voice was unmistakeable. Deep and smooth like rolling thunder.

The three-fingered man had found them.

>>>———→

Bron was reacting before the Viking had even finished his sentence. He turned, dropped, and raised his bow in one fluid motion. Ylva hadn't known it was possible to move with such speed. But he wasn't fast enough. As Bron reached to take an arrow from his quiver, the flame-haired woman appeared like a ghost from the shadow of the stable. Firelight glimmered on the short iron sword in her fist as she took two great strides forward and brought the pommel down hard on the side of Bron's head.

Bron's legs buckled and he collapsed like a sack of

grain. He didn't even make a sound.

'You should give me your axe.' The three-fingered man stepped from the shadow to stand behind the woman. He looked Ylva in the eye and held out his hand. 'Unless you want her to hit you too.'

The Three-Fingered Man

39

Bound

The three-fingered man sat on a stool by the stable door. Ylva's axe lay across his lap. He was blowing into a bone flute, trying to make something that sounded like music, but it was spoilt by his lack of fingers.

Sitting on the stable floor, Ylva's wrists were bound with rough hemp rope. Another length of rope ran from her wrists and was fastened around her neck. Her heart was still pounding, and emotions surged through her. Fear, hate, anger, frustration, all of them boiling together like poison in her veins. She dug the fingernails of her right hand hard into the skin on the back of her left hand, trying to clear her mind. She had to find a way out of this. The gods wanted revenge, so they would show her how; she had to be ready for their sign.

'You like music?' The deep, rumbling voice was familiar, but Ylva had never been this close to him. He had removed his helmet and she could see the pores on his bald head, and the shape of each rune tattooed into his skin. She could see the cracks in the black kohl that ringed his ice-blue eyes, every bristle on his chin, and every individual hair in the wolfskins he wore. She could smell the wild and filthy scent that came off him.

'My name is Torstein Ulvemand.' The stool creaked as he placed the flute on the floor beside him and rested both hands on the axe across his lap.

Torstein Ulvemand. The three-fingered man had a name.

'Have you heard of me?' he asked.

'No.'

A flash of disappointment crossed his face before he showed her a tight-lipped smile. 'This is Astrid.' He gestured at the flame-haired woman without taking his eyes off Ylva's. 'And you are . . . ?'

'I don't care to tell you. I don't intend to make a friend of you.'

'I see. Well, I know nothing about you except that you've been riding with a pair of murdering thieves and –' he nodded at Freki, now leashed to one of the stable posts – 'a wolf pup?'

'Definitely a wolf pup.' Astrid was settling their horses, stabling them beside the chestnut that had brought Bron to Seatun. Freki was at her feet, but didn't seem bothered by her. He was curled in the straw, watching her with his chin on his paws. Ylva felt betrayed by his lack of hate for the slavers.

She looked down at Bron beside her, bound in the same way she was. Instead of sitting, though, he was lying curled with his eyes closed. One side of his face was thick with congealed blood.

'He's not dead,' the woman said. 'I didn't hit him that hard.'

'He'll live.' The three-fingered man put his right hand to his mouth as if he was thinking. Where the two smallest fingers should have been, there were just two stumps. 'That woman you left up in the cave is dead though. It's a shame. She stole something valuable from me, and I wanted to make her pay for it.'

'The boy will have to do.' The flame-haired woman glanced over her shoulder as she took the bags from her horse. 'It took us a long time to find that cave you were hiding in.' She loosened the saddle and removed it as she spoke. 'We had to split up and ride around in circles for a day at least. The snow covered your tracks almost as soon as you laid them, but we found it in the end.' She looked over at Ylva as she took blankets from the horse's back and draped them over the stall fence. 'We found the woman, and enough good signs to know you were heading in this direction. We were going to camp down for the night but—'

'We saw your fire.' The three-fingered man finished her sentence. 'You made things easy for us in the end.' He fixed Ylva with his ice-blue eyes.

Ylva ignored him and glanced around for something to use as a weapon, but there wasn't much in the stable other than straw. The only useful things were Bron's bow leaning against the door, and her own axe lying across the three-fingered man's lap. But even if she were fast enough to take them – which she wasn't – she'd never manage it while tied like an animal.

She would find a way to survive, though, she was determined. The rope would not be around her neck for long.

The three-fingered man put his hand back on the axe, and while the woman finished settling her own horse and started on his, he drummed the two fingers of his right hand on the broadest part of the axe blade. His nails tapped the iron as he studied Ylva.

Ting-ting. Ting-ting . . . He stopped. 'Who are you? From the way you talk, I'd say you're a Dane, but what are you doing with this boy? Are you a slave?'

'I'm not a slave. My father is a jarl from Jorvik. He's a berserker with an army of a hundred men, so you should let me go now or—'

'You're a bad liar.' The woman came to stand beside the three-fingered man. 'And you *are* a slave. Those marks on your neck are from a collar. Who do you belong to?'

'I'm not a slave.' Ylva stared at her, unable to hide her hatred. The last time Ylva had seen this woman, she was putting Mother's locket around her neck. And now Ylva could see the locket again, hanging against the woman's tunic; the same locket she had stolen from Mother's body.

In that moment, Ylva's need for revenge was like a fist of ice crushing her heart. She had never felt anything like it – not even when she had found Mother lying dead in the trader's hut – and she wanted to leap at the woman like a wild animal, to tear the locket from her, and make her pay for what she had done. She wanted to—

Stay calm.

The voice echoed in her head and, just when she needed him, Geri was there, sitting by the door with his ears pricked up and his nose in her direction.

Stay calm and survive. Don't let them know who you are.

She dug her nails harder into her skin and bit the inside of her cheek to keep herself thinking straight. Geri was right; she had to be calm. She had to survive. 'If you do anything to hurt me, my father will find you and kill you.' Her teeth were clamped together so tight that her mouth barely moved.

'Like you want to kill me?' the three-fingered man asked. 'I heard you say that outside. Why do you want to kill me?'

The words were in her mouth, but Ylva stopped herself from saying them. If she told him about Mother and Geri, about her revenge, he might kill her right now where she sat. The three-fingered man was a Dane – a Viking – he would understand the importance of revenge. He would know what it meant to Ylva, and how far she would go to get it.

When she said nothing, the three-fingered man narrowed his eyes. 'Tell me then – if you're not a slave, what are you doing with this boy?' He nodded his head at Bron.

'He helped me. Your men in the forest were going to kill me.'

The three-fingered man leant forward. 'You're talking

about Halvor and his brothers? You think they were going to kill you?' He widened his eyes and tilted his head. 'And then I suppose they were going to eat you? Arvid would have liked that. Did you see his teeth?' He opened his mouth and ran the tip of his tongue over his own teeth. 'He said all those sharp points were perfect for gnawing on the bones of small children.' He snapped his jaws at Ylva, making her recoil in horror.

The three-fingered man smiled and shook his head at her. 'Vikings don't eat children – you're too valuable. Selling you is much better than eating you.'

'We might even sell him instead of just killing him.' The flame-haired woman pointed at Bron. 'It might make up for all the silver we've lost and the time we've wasted. We've been hunting them for weeks.'

'Weeks?' Ylva tried to make sense of that. The three-fingered man had been hunting them for *weeks*? She let it sink in as she realized what it meant.

You were wrong, Geri said. *The half-skulls weren't hunting you. They were hunting Cathryn and Bron. They had been hunting them long before we even arrived at the trader's hut.*

Ylva looked up at the three-fingered man. 'You were already hunting them? Before they killed those men at the camp?'

'Yes.'

'Why?'

'Because they stole from me.' The three-fingered man spat the words at Ylva. 'They stole my slaves.'

'Your slaves?' It was almost too much for Ylva to think about.

'One last raid outside Jorvik and we would have had

enough.' The woman glared at Bron. 'But he and that woman stole them.'

'Your slaves?' Ylva said again. Everything was upside down and muddled in her head, and she couldn't quite grasp it. 'I don't . . . Why would they steal your slaves?'

'To sell, of course. What else would they do with them? They're slavers, like me. They probably planned to sell you too.'

40

Murderous Thieves

Ylva didn't know what to think any more. Could she really have been so wrong about Cathryn?

It can't be true. I don't believe it.

Ylva looked into the shadow at the corner of the stable and saw Geri sitting in the darkness, eyes shining as he watched her.

It can't be true.

Ylva had never seen him more clearly. Never wanted so much for him to be there with her.

'I don't believe it either,' she said to him before looking at Bron lying beside her. 'I don't believe it.' Ylva hadn't known Cathryn and Bron for long, but she couldn't imagine they would steal and sell slaves. It didn't make sense. 'Cathryn said slavery was wrong.' She turned to the three-fingered man. 'Bron cut off my collar.'

'Tricks to make you trust them.' The woman shrugged. 'Make you do as they said.'

'They *helped* me.'

'They *fooled* you.' The three-fingered man raised his voice. 'Accept it.' He fixed his eyes on Ylva as if they might cut right through her. 'Now, go and make us something to eat. I'm starving and it's going to be a long night. There's food in there.' He made an impatient gesture with his hand and pointed to a bundle by the wall. 'Make something hot.'

Ylva stared at him, unable to think. Unable to move. She was numb inside. Could she really have been so wrong? Had she come all this way just to be a slave for a new owner?

'Do it now!' The three-fingered man growled.

It was difficult to manage with her wrists tied to the short rope around her neck, but Ylva struggled to her feet. She glanced at Bron, still lying on the straw. He hadn't moved and she wondered if he was going to die, but for a second his eyes flickered and he looked at her. It was almost too fast to see, but long enough to let her know he was awake.

And now Geri was sitting right beside him. *You have to think clearly. Trust Bron. Get them to untie you.*

'I can't cook anything like this.' Ylva held her hands up as much as she could. 'You'll have to untie me.'

'I don't think so,' the flame-haired woman said.

'Do it,' the three-fingered man told her. 'I haven't eaten all day, and what harm can she do? You think she'll try to kill us? She's a child, what does she know about killing?'

'There isn't a Dane that doesn't know about killing,' the woman said.

The three-fingered man snorted. 'But she's so small. Untie her.'

The flame-haired woman hesitated, then came forward and loosened the rope. She wound it into a coil and threw it down on the floor close to the three-fingered man. 'You cook; I'll make a fire. But as soon as you're done, the rope goes back on.'

Ylva went to the bundle by the wall. She lifted a cloak to reveal a basket made from woven beech rods. It had loops on each side so a person could carry it over their back. When she opened the top, she saw among other things: an iron cooking pot, chunks of fresh wild boar wrapped in cloth and an assortment of vegetables. While she took out what she needed, the woman scraped a shallow pit in the centre of the stable and filled it with coals collected from the smouldering remains of the workshop outside.

Ylva banged the pot down directly on to the fire so that sparks flew up around it. She splashed water into it and threw in the meat and the vegetables. The three-fingered man wouldn't allow her a knife to cut them, so she snapped the parsnips and carrots, imagining they were his bones. She tore the cabbage to shreds, vowing that this would be the last meal she would ever cook as a slave.

Sitting on her haunches to work, Ylva glanced over her shoulder. The three-fingered man was still on the stool, but he had put Ylva's axe on the floor beside the bone flute. He was facing the flame-haired woman, who was perched on an upturned wooden bucket. Deep in conversation, both of them had taken the weapons from their belts and leant them against the wall. They were out of Ylva's reach but as she stirred the wooden spoon and looked down into the blackened pot, an idea began to form.

When she was sure the Vikings weren't watching her, Ylva nudged Bron to get his attention. He opened his eyes just enough to acknowledge her, and she used her hands to tell him what she planned to do. She didn't know the hand-speak he used with Cathryn, but she did her best, and eventually he nodded and closed his eyes.

As soon as he did, Ylva took the wooden spoon out of the pot and placed the handle into the fire. She shuffled round to make sure the three-fingered man and the flame-haired woman couldn't see the spoon handle begin to burn.

Ylva stared into the pot, watching the meat and vegetables turning, rising, falling in the water. It was like her mind – all those thoughts muddling together.

'. . . ready?' the woman asked.

'Hm?' Ylva looked back at her. 'What?'

'I said is the food ready? My stomach's as empty as a poor man's treasure chest.'

'Almost.' Ylva pushed the cluttered thoughts from her mind and focused on one thing. This was her best chance, her only chance, to avenge Mother. She held the burning wooden spoon by the wide end and took it from the fire. Blowing out the flame, she turned her body so the Vikings couldn't see her press the glowing end of the spoon to the rope binding Bron's hands. It took only a few seconds to burn through the hemp and free him.

'Yes,' she said as she tossed the spoon into the fire. 'It's done.' She picked up the cloth that had been wrapped around the boar meat, and glanced across at Bron. He nodded just enough to show that he was ready.

'Well, bring it over here, child. I'm itching to find out if your stew is as bitter as your personality,' said the three-fingered man.

'As long as it's better than your flute playing.' Ylva used the cloth to protect her hands as she lifted the pot from the fire and, moving as quickly as she could, she turned and took three paces towards the Vikings. And when she was directly in front of them, Ylva hurled the scalding stew into their faces.

Bron was on his feet as the Vikings flinched away, turning their heads and raising their hands, but they were too late to protect themselves. Ylva had never heard a grown man scream until the moment red-hot stew splashed into the three-fingered man's eyes, and she was quick to take advantage of his pain.

41

Sharp Iron

Ylva was on him like a wolf on its prey. She threw all her weight against him, pushing him backwards off the stool. Any difficulty she had being close to other people was forgotten as she grabbed his head with both hands and hit it once, twice, against the floor.

Everything inside the stable was in chaos. The horses huffed and stamped their hooves, Bron struggled with the flame-haired woman, and by the stalls, Freki leapt up to strain at his leash, and bark as best as he could.

The whites of the three-fingered man's eyes were now red, burnt by the boiling stew, and they rolled in confusion and pain. But he was as strong as a bear, and no stranger to battle. Ylva was no match for his strength. When she turned to stretch for her axe lying close by, he came to his senses and reached up with both hands to grab her around the neck. He pushed her back with all his strength, squeezing his hands together, trying to crush the life from her.

Ylva twisted from side to side, hammering one fist against the three-fingered man, hitting his chest, scratching at his face and eyes as she scrabbled blindly with her other hand, trying to lay her fingers on the axe. But the three-fingered man had a grip like Fenrir's jaws. With his hands still around her neck, he lifted her off his chest and threw her sideways to land on her back with a bone-jarring thump.

The impact knocked the breath out of her, but she reached out again, desperate as her fingertips brushed against the leather binding on the lower part of the handle. There it was. Her axe. The same axe she had used to defeat the bear. She would use it now, to split the three-fingered man's skull. All she had to do was take hold of it and—

The three-fingered man sat up and grabbed Ylva by the arm, dragging her towards him, out of reach of the axe. As soon as she was close, he got to his knees and lifted her so she was sitting with her back against his chest, then he wrapped both arms around her neck. 'I'll break it if I have to,' he said in her ear. 'But don't make me kill you. You're a brave one, and I'll get a good price for you.'

The pressure on her neck constricted her throat and made her head pound. She heard the blood thumping in her veins and her face grew numb as everything darkened. He was squeezing the breath out of her, but all she could think of was avenging Mother. Of killing the three-fingered man. Of killing the woman and taking back the locket. She had a duty. The gods expected it of her. And if she were to fail, she would die trying. It was too late to give up now.

As her vision began to fade, Ylva frantically reached out sideways with both hands, running her fingers through the straw, searching for a weapon. Searching and hoping and searching until her fingers brushed against something hard and she shifted her eyes to see one of Bron's arrows lying in the dirt. Without thinking, she took it in her fist and thrust it backwards with all the strength she had left in her, driving it hard into the three-fingered man's side.

The three-fingered man cried out in pain and let go, giving Ylva the chance to shuffle forward and turn around to face him.

His was on his knees looking down in confusion at the arrow sticking out beneath his ribs. 'How did you—?'

Ylva put both hands around the shaft of the arrow and pushed as hard as she could.

Truth

42

Revenge

The three-fingered man looked up at Ylva standing over him with her axe. He tried to move, but he was weak and couldn't do anything more than turn his head. 'The gods are playing with me.' There was blood on his teeth. 'Beaten by a child.'

'I'm not a child,' Ylva said. 'And I'll tell you what I know about killing. I know that you killed my mother . . . and my dog. So now I'm going to kill you.'

'Your mother?' The three-fingered man closed his eyes and took a deep, wheezing breath.

'You murdered her.' Ylva's voice caught in her throat. 'You and that woman.' Ylva was here now. At last. After all this time and struggle, she was finally bringing her promise to the three-fingered man. Bringing her revenge. And now she longed for the expected feelings of relief and satisfaction, a sense of justice being done. But she felt none of those things. She felt only grief and exhaustion and emptiness. Here he was, lying at her feet, ready to die, but Mother and Geri were still dead, and nothing she could do – not even killing this man – would bring them back. Nothing was different.

'You killed them.' Ylva's voice came as a shouted whisper. 'You killed them.' She tried to make her muscles work, to strike him dead, but something deep inside wouldn't let her do it. She couldn't kill him. She had come all this way, struggled so hard, and now she couldn't even do what she had come here to do.

She relaxed her arm and let the weapon hang by her side. 'I hate you. Why can't I kill you?'

'You already have. You put this arrow in me.'

'It feels different.'

'Because you were fighting. Protecting yourself. Killing a man in cold blood is different. It shouldn't be easy. The gods don't like it.'

'Even if it's revenge?' Ylva looked down at him. When she had first seen him, he was a monster, but now he was just a man; crippled and dying.

His breath came in shallow sips, his chest hitching with each one. 'I've killed my share of men, but I've never killed a woman. Not once.'

Ylva stared at him.

'I swear an oath to the All-Father,' he whispered.

'That trader's hut,' Ylva said. 'You left a dead woman and . . . and a dog . . .'

The three-fingered man frowned and coughed flecks of blood into his beard.

'And she stole Mother's locket.' Ylva looked over at the flame-haired woman lying on her back, with one arm stretched out, and the other twisted beneath her. Two arrow shafts protruded from the centre of her chest.

Bron sat beside her, with his bow still in his hands. He was slumped in exhaustion, eyes half-closed as he watched Ylva standing over the Viking.

The three-fingered man took a long, laboured breath and nodded his head. 'Oh. That.' There was sadness in his eyes as he looked at the woman lying in the straw, her hair splayed out as Mother's had been. 'I told Astrid to leave it.' He sighed. 'But you should know I didn't kill your mother. The owner of the hut did that.'

'What? Don't lie.'

'Your mother went into that hut to steal blankets and food.'

'She went in there to trade.'

'No. She had nothing to trade so she went in there to steal. To keep you and her alive. I saw it with my own eyes. But it went wrong for her. The owner got the better of her and killed her. When the dog tried to protect her, he killed that too.' He coughed again and shook his head. 'Where you and I come from, murder is a crime – even worse than stealing another man's slaves – and it needs to be paid with blood or silver, so I killed him. For the gods.'

'You're lying.'

'Child, I'm ready for Valhalla.' He closed his eyes. 'I have no reason to save myself from you. Odin sees all; he knows the truth. I avenged your mother for you. The Viking way. The man who killed her is already dead.'

43

Locket

Ylva didn't help the three-fingered man when he shuffled over to prop himself against the wall, but she didn't stop him either. Instead, she gathered all the weapons and put them out of his reach, then went to the flame-haired woman and pulled down her collar to take the locket from around her neck.

It was not a valuable locket. It was not made from silver or gold, and it didn't hang on a delicate necklace. It was carved from a piece of ash wood and hung from a leather cord. Mother once told Ylva she had carved the coin-shaped locket from wood taken from a branch of Yggdrasil, the ash tree that protected and sheltered all nine worlds. For a while, Ylva had even believed her. A blackened image of Thor's hammer was burnt on to the front of the locket. Ylva remembered when Mother had made the mark, saying that she chose the hammer because although Odin was the All-Father, he was the god for warriors and jarls. Thor was the god who protected common people. Thor stood for justice.

The locket contained two twists of hair, both of them taken from the heads of people she had never really known; her father and her sister. They were slaves who had died from fever before Ylva could even talk, and when she took the twists in her fingertips and tried to feel a connection to those people, she felt nothing. She had no idea what they looked like or how their voices sounded.

She placed the locket on the dead woman's chest and untied a pouch from her belt. From inside the pouch, she removed the two locks of hair she had taken in the hut; one from Mother's head, and one from Geri's coat. When she put them to her nose, they smelt of nothing, but she felt closer to those they had belonged to. She saw Mother's face and heard her voice, but in time that would fade from her memory and they would just be locks of hair.

Ylva put her family in the locket and snapped it shut. She hung it around her neck and looked at Bron sitting slumped beside the woman.

'Are you hurt?' she asked.

Bron reached into his cloak. When he took his hand out again, it was covered with blood.

44

Valhalla

Ylva dragged Bron over to the wall and sat him beside the three-fingered man. She loosened Freki's leash and gathered him in her arms before she collapsed beside Bron and stared into what was left of the fire.

The air grew steadily colder.

You were wrong about everything, Geri said.

Ylva didn't look up to see him sitting in the shadow. She didn't want to think about it, but what he said was true. She had been wrong about why Mother went into the trader's hut, and she had been wrong about who had killed her. She had even been wrong about why the three-fingered man had been tracking her. And maybe – *maybe* – she had been wrong about Cathryn and Bron too. Had they really been planning to sell her, like the three-fingered man had said?

So much had happened, but nothing had changed. The man who murdered Mother and Geri was dead, but it didn't make any difference to anything. Ylva didn't feel better. Sadness and anger still flooded her veins, pumping through her body as if they were the only things keeping her alive. Tears threatened to well in her eyes and spill down her cheeks, but she bit them back and refused to let them come. There was a time for tears, Mother had told her, but this wasn't the time.

'You came a long way to find out the truth,' the three-fingered man muttered. 'And revenge is a heavy thing to carry with you. Dangerous too. It always turns around to bite you.' He closed his eyes and laughed quietly. 'You're one tough little girl, but you came all this way for the wrong man.'

Ylva turned to look at him; at the arrow lodged under his ribs.

'And I came all this way to be killed by a child.' His throat rattled as he tried to laugh. 'If I'd known, I would've just found some more slaves, gone back to my ship in Jorvik, and sailed away. Taken my chances with the winter seas. But I chased after the thieves, and the gods put an arrow in me. That's revenge for you.'

'I put it there, not the gods,' Ylva said. 'I could pull it out if you want.'

'No.' He shook his head. 'It's probably the only thing keeping me from bleeding to death.'

Beside Ylva, Bron slowly took his right hand from beneath the cloak. With effort, he spiralled his finger above his head, and ran the claw of his hand down his hair as if he was combing it.

'I don't understand,' Ylva said.

Bron continued to make the hand-speak. He repeated the same movements but they were sluggish and painful.

'I'm sorry,' Ylva said. 'I still don't know what you're trying to tell me.'

Bron took a deep breath. 'Witch.'

'Witch? You're calling me . . . oh. You mean *the* Witch,' Ylva said. 'The one Cathryn told me about. She can help?'

Bron nodded.

'Is she close?'

Bron held up one finger.

'A day to get there?'

He nodded.

'Do you know the way?'

He nodded again.

Ylva got to her feet and went to the door. She pulled it open and looked up at the sky, but the clouds were thick and she could see no moon or stars. It would be too difficult to travel – too dangerous. 'We'll set off at first light,' she said. 'I'll build up the fire to keep us warm until then.'

'You'll save him, even though he wants to sell you?' The three-fingered man watched her.

'I don't believe that,' Ylva said.

'You mean you don't *want* to believe it. Anyway, the boy will need more than a fire to keep him alive.'

'He'll live,' Ylva told him.

'I'm not so sure. Shame. He's worth a lot of silver.'

Ylva grabbed her axe and held it in her fist. She pointed it at the three-fingered man. 'You might not have done what I thought you did, but I still don't like you. You're a slaver, and you were hunting my friends. If you make me angry, I might change my mind about killing you.'

'You haven't got it in you,' he mumbled. 'But I'll probably be in Valhalla by morning anyway.'

'I can only hope.' Ylva replied.

45

One Last Time

Ylva gathered wood from the huts in the village and rekindled the fire in the stable. Remembering what had happened in the workshop, she was careful to clear the dry straw from the area around the fire. When that was done, she laid out furs and blankets for Bron and the three-fingered man so they weren't lying on the cold ground. She made them as comfortable as she could. She covered the flame-haired woman with a blanket, and sat staring into the fire.

Freki huddled in the folds of her cloak and closed his eyes while Ylva stroked his fur and enjoyed the gentle rise and fall of his soft belly.

For a strange moment – the first since coming to England – Ylva felt at home. The warm, sweet smell of the horses. The feel of the straw. The glow of the fire. At home, Ylva had often slept in the stable with the horses, she and Mother curled in the straw, with Geri lying against her. Ylva had been born a slave, she had never known different, but her owner had not been as bad as others. Some owners beat their slaves, made them sleep with pigs, but Ylva remembered fresh straw and warm fires. She remembered laughter and voices from the great hall. Many nights, she and Mother would sit at the stable door, watching the stars and wondering what it would be like to be free. But now she *was* free, she would have given anything to be back at home in the stable with Mother, watching the stars.

➤

As the night drew on, Ylva kept the fire burning. The horses nickered behind her. Freki climbed from her lap and sniffed around the stable, so Ylva tied his leash to a stable post, to stop him from exploring further than his rope would allow. Ylva kept herself awake by telling Bron and the three-fingered man about her journey, and her life at home. She imagined she was a skald, telling the saga of Ylva the Fearless, though she was sure neither of them was listening to her.

She cleaned Bron's wound with warm water made from snow melted over the fire. She cut the half-skull scarf from around Torstein Ulvemand's neck and packed it against Bron's wound. 'Please don't die,' she whispered as she worked, but there was never any sign that Bron could hear her.

➤

That night, the wolves returned to Ylva one last time. The first she knew of it was when Freki whined and jumped to his feet, and the horses spooked, snorting and flaring their nostrils.

Ylva was about to throw wood on to the fire, but she stopped and listened to the endless dark outside.

Freki strained against his leash. The horses turned on the spot and grew more agitated.

'Easy,' Ylva whispered to them. 'Easy.' She dropped the damp wood on to the fire and went to the horses, speaking softly to keep them calm. 'Do you hear something?' she asked them. 'What do you hear out there?'

But even if horses could talk, they wouldn't have needed to tell Ylva what was out there, because a howl cut through the night.

Ylva's scalp tingled. She was more afraid now than she had been in the workshop. There, at least she'd had Bron to give her courage. But now Bron was in the deep sleep of the dying, and Ylva was alone. She gripped her axe and went to the door, opening it enough to look out.

A shaft of orange firelight spilt out across the snow, but beyond it, the night was as dark as Hel's heart.

'Easy,' she murmured to the horses. 'It's all right.'

But the horses weren't convinced. They jittered from side to side. They rolled their eyes and swivelled their ears.

Freki, too, was agitated. He whined and pulled harder at his rope.

Ylva listened to the night. She listened beyond the snorts of the horses, trying to hear the soft pad of paws in the snow, but she heard nothing as the large beast emerged like a spirit from the endless night. It stole into the edge of the shaft of light, flames flickering in its amber eyes. With its coat of black fur, Ylva knew at once it was the same animal she had seen before.

A second and third wolf materialized from the darkness on either side of it. These two were lighter in colour, lean and tall with muscular shoulders. They moved with their heads low, their eyes alert. Other shapes moved backwards and forwards in the shadows.

The horses were frantic now. Freki was dancing at the end of his lead, whining and pulling so hard he might choke himself.

Ylva heaved the door open and raised the axe as she shouted.

'Get away! Leave us alone!'

Taken by surprise, the lighter-coloured wolves turned and disappeared into the darkness, but the black wolf stayed where it was. It flinched and bared its teeth, but it didn't take so much as a step back.

'Get away!' Ylva shouted again. 'Leave us alone.' She dared to move towards it, brandishing the axe, but the wolf stood its ground.

'Go on!' Ylva shouted. 'Leave!'

Freki pulled against his leash. The horses snorted.

The wolf growled.

'Leave us alone!'

'Ylva.' The voice was quieter than a whisper. At first she thought it was the wolf that had spoken her name. It took her a second to realize it was Bron, and she turned to look at him lying with his eyes half-open.

'Freki.' He raised his right hand and pointed at the wolf pup. 'Let. Him. Go.'

'They'll kill him,' she said.

'No.'

'I won't let him go. He's mine.' But in her heart, Ylva knew Freki wasn't hers. Freki was wild and free, and the rope didn't belong around his neck any more than an iron collar belonged around hers.

She watched the black wolf standing at the edge of the light, baring its teeth, then she looked at Freki, straining at his rope.

'Let. Him. Go,' Bron said.

Ylva stepped back into the stable and sank to her knees beside the pup. She hugged him once and kissed the top of his head, then loosened the rope and lifted it from around his neck.

'Good luck,' she said to him. 'Be free.'

When she let go of him, Freki scampered out of the stable towards the black wolf. He danced around its legs, the pair of them snapping at each other's muzzles. Freki ran circles around the larger animal, yipping and huffing. He came back to Ylva, ran around her legs, then returned to the edge of the shaft of firelight.

When the large black wolf retreated into the darkness and disappeared from view, Freki followed.

Ylva stood for a long time, waiting for him to come back, but she never saw Freki again.

46

Ylva the Strong

Ylva fed the fire and tended the horses. She sat cross-legged beside Bron, knowing it was too dark and too dangerous to ride on, but thinking it was too dangerous not to. Bron was burning with fever, like Cathryn had been, and as Ylva listened to his breathing she became certain of one thing.

If she waited until dawn, Bron would die.

'No.' She got to her feet. 'I won't let that happen.'

Ylva saddled Bron's horse and packed it with supplies. She gathered the weapons from the stable floor and secured them behind the saddle before shaking Bron awake. 'I need to get you to the Witch.'

Bron looked at her as if he didn't know who she was or where they were.

'I'm Ylva. You remember me? Friend.' She hooked her

fingers together, as he had shown her. 'Friend. I'm going to help you.'

The boy hardly had any strength in him. He was pale and weak, and struggled to keep his eyes open. He shivered from more than just the cold. Fever was taking him the same way it had taken Cathryn. She had to hurry.

Ylva pulled him to his feet and half walked, half dragged him to the horse. At least he was lean and light, which made it possible to shove him up on to the animal's back and slide him to the front of the saddle. She put the reins in his hands and rested him forward on to the horse's neck to stop him from falling.

Satisfied that Bron was secure, she pulled the stable door wide, letting the cold wind blow a flurry of snow inside. She went to the horse, about to climb on, but stopped and looked back at the three-fingered man. She went to him and kicked him in the leg. 'We're leaving.'

Torstein Ulvemand's eyes rolled. 'Is it still dark? It's still dark, isn't it?'

'I have to go. You're on your own now.'

He couldn't focus on her face. He turned his head from side to side, trying to clear his thoughts. 'It's you.' His breath came in short, wheezing gasps. 'You're still here. You should've . . . gone with the wolves. You'd get on with them.'

'For a while I thought you were Ulfhednar,' Ylva said to him. 'The wolfskins and the howling and the half-skulls made me so afraid of you, but I'm not afraid of you now. You're Torstein Ulvemand. You're not Ulfhednar, you're just a man. And not a good one.'

Ylva crossed the stable and climbed into the saddle

behind Bron. She nudged the horse towards the stable door, ready to ride into the night.

'Give me my sword,' Torstein said as she passed him. 'Put it in my hand. Let me die as a warrior and take my place in Valhalla.'

Ylva stopped the horse and looked down at him. 'It's too valuable. I might need it to pay the Witch.'

'Your knife then? Your axe?'

Ylva put her hand to the axe on her belt. 'I'm sorry, Torstein Ulvemand.'

'Then an arrow will have to do.' Torstein reached down and wrapped his huge fist around the shaft of the arrow in his side. He looked directly into Ylva's eyes. 'You came all this way. The cold. Wolves. Bears.' There was blood on his lips. 'Ylva the Fearless.'

'I thought you weren't listening.'

'But . . . I don't think . . . you're fearless . . .' he said. 'I think . . . you're strong. Strongest person I ever met. Good luck, Ylva the Strong. May the gods favour you.'

The three-fingered man closed his eyes, put back his head, and pulled the arrow from his side.

Ylva didn't stay to watch him stop breathing.

47

Bron

Bron sat in the saddle in front of Ylva, so she could keep him from falling. He indicated the direction they needed to go and Ylva pushed the horse as fast as she dared. She wanted to kick it into a gallop, to make it fly, but she had to let it find the safest path.

The travelling was slow and they moved through the forest like explorers discovering it for the first time.

At first light, they finally broke from the trees. The clouds had lifted, and the sun was a welcome sight, making its daily journey across the sky. It brought no warmth, but at least it chased away the unbearable darkness. Ylva pushed on endlessly across a vast plain of deep snow until she found herself on the bank of a river that was too wide and too fast to cross. On the opposite side of the water lay the stone ruins of ancient buildings and walls, the like of which she had never seen before.

Bron was slumped forward on the horse, with his eyes closed. Ylva nudged him awake. 'Which way now?'

He took so long to open his eyes that Ylva wondered if he had died.

'Which way?' She nudged him again. 'Bron? Which way?'

Bron lifted a hand and pointed east along the riverbank, so Ylva set off again.

Cold and exhausted, she struggled to keep the boy in the saddle, but soon a familiar salty scent was in the air again, and by early afternoon she at last reached the place where the river met the sea. From her vantage point over the beach, Ylva looked out across the waves, and her heart lifted at the sight of the craggy island lying just off the coast. It was nothing like she had expected, not at all the kind of place where she imagined a witch would live, but she knew this must be where Cathryn and Bron had wanted her to come.

The teardrop island had no beaches, just black, jagged cliffs. The only way on or off was along a narrow causeway – hardly even wide enough for a cart – that led from the beach to a large wooden gate on the nearside of the island. On either side of the gate, high timber walls circled the clifftop, with a walkway running the whole circumference. Ylva counted eight warriors posted around the fence, where they had a perfect view of land and sea.

Within the walls, a circle of wooden huts was built around a large grey stone building with a tower where two more warriors stood guard. The barley and moss thatch over the buildings was almost completely clear of snow, indicating they were warm inside. Outside the circle of houses, around the edge of the high fence, there was a sturdy barn for horses, and areas cleared for winter vegetables. There were animals, too – chickens and pigs in their own pens.

From where she watched, Ylva saw adults and children moving among the houses, tending to the crops and animals as if it were an ordinary village, but she knew she wasn't looking at an ordinary village. This was an island fortress. The people who lived here had found a place that was protected from all sides – even from the shallow-draught boats of Viking raiders.

Ylva longed to be inside the fortress, but something made her hesitate. Saxons would populate the island – the same race that had attacked and slaughtered her people when they landed on the beach all those days ago. A Saxon had killed Mother and Geri. Saxons hated Vikings. If Ylva approached the island, would Saxons kill her too?

Cathryn was a Saxon.

Ylva kept her eyes on the island, but she imagined Geri sitting beside her horse. She pictured him with his head up, his ears pricked forward, and his mouth open. His tongue was out to taste the salt in the air, and his black and grey fur was ruffling in the cold breeze that came off the sea.

You could trust Cathryn. This is where she wanted you to come. You'll be safe here.

48

The Witch

Descending towards the beach, Ylva heard the lyrical ring of a bell chiming within the hollow crash of waves. One of the lookouts on the island must have spotted her approach and sounded the alarm. There was now a flurry of activity among the buildings, people running to gather children and keep out of sight, others taking up arms and making for the walls.

Ylva braced herself for attack as she crossed the sand and urged the horse on to the slippery causeway. The sea smashed the rocks either side of her, spraying her with icy water, engulfing the path before drawing away and leaving seaweed strewn in its wake.

She kept her eyes on the figures standing on the wall nearest the gate and held out her arms to show she meant no harm. Halfway across the causeway, she realized the sea was now swirling around the horse's hooves and not receding. If anything it was becoming deeper, and to those watching from the wall it might have seemed as if she were riding across the surface of the water.

Shocked, Ylva grabbed the reins and nudged the horse to move faster. At this rate, the ground would be gone in just a few minutes.

As she reached the front gate, Ylva brought the horse to a halt and looked up at the warriors on the wall. She expected them to be men but was surprised to see four women, dressed in leather and mail, each of them aiming a bow at her.

'Stop there! Who are you?' one of them shouted down to her.

'I need help,' Ylva shouted back. 'Cathryn sent me.'

'You're a Dane.' The women exchanged glances, before the one who had spoken to her called down again. 'Who are you? What do you want?'

More women came to join them, looking out towards the beach, scanning the shore.

'Are you alone?' they asked.

'Cathryn sent me,' Ylva yelled over the crashing of waves. 'I have Bron. Please.' The water was around the horse's fetlocks now, approaching his knees. Before long it would be touching his belly. 'Let us in.'

'Where's Cathryn?'

'Gone,' Ylva said. 'Please! Let us in.' She grabbed the back of Bron's tunic and pulled him up so his head lolled back and his face was towards the sky. 'He needs help!' Ylva frantically looked around at the deepening water. 'Please!'

The women spoke among themselves, words that were lost in the roar of breakers smashing against the island, then one of them leant to the side and shouted down. 'Let them in!'

A moment later, the gate drew back and Ylva's horse surged forward without encouragement. It waded across the end of the causeway and stepped up on to the island.

As soon as Ylva was on dry land, two women pushed the gate closed. Beyond it, the causeway was now completely submerged.

'Good thing you came across when you did, child.' One of the gatekeepers came to take the reins of Ylva's horse and steady it. She wore a mail vest and carried a spear in her left hand. 'If you'd tried it a few moments later, the sea would've had you.' Her long hair blew in the wind. 'What happened to Bron?'

'He's hurt,' Ylva said. 'I need the Witch. Where is she?'

'She's up at the abbey.' The woman pointed to the large, grey stone building in the centre of the island. 'I'll take—'

Ylva dug her heels into the horse's flanks and the reins tore out of the woman's hands.

'Hey!'

Ylva ignored the shouts and galloped towards the centre of the island. When she came closer to the abbey, the front door opened, and an old woman stepped out. She wore a plain linen dress with a woollen cloak wrapped around her shoulders. Long grey hair was pulled up to the top of her head and tied in an untidy twist. She rested one hand on her hip as she watched Ylva approach. A mangy grey dog slipped out behind her and started barking, but the old woman ignored it.

Ylva jumped down from the horse and reached up for Bron. 'Help him,' she said to the old woman.

The boy had no strength at all. He slipped sideways, and Ylva took as much of his weight as she could to soften his fall into the snow. 'Help him!' Ylva turned and shouted at the old woman. 'Please.'

Every inch of the old woman's skin was wrinkled like a dried riverbed, and her brown, watery eyes were set deep. Her lips were so thin they were hardly even there.

There was a flurry of movement as warriors formed a semicircle behind Ylva, brandishing swords and spears. 'Stop there! Stay where you are!'

But Ylva didn't even look back to acknowledge them. 'He's hurt.' She took Bron under the shoulders and dragged him towards the old stone abbey. 'Please. Why won't you help me?'

'Bron!' A younger woman hurried out from the hall and came straight to help Ylva. 'What happened to him?' She took hold of Bron's feet. 'Mother, get out of the way. And one of you come and help me.'

The old woman stepped aside, and one of the warriors came forward, but Ylva refused to let them help as she and the young woman carried Bron into the warmth of the abbey.

'It's bad,' Ylva said as they took him to a room at the back and put him on a straw-covered bed. The dog followed, sniffing at the wounded boy, so the woman shooed it back out into the main room. It went to the fire and collapsed in a curled heap.

'What happened to him?' The woman ran her fingers along Bron's cheek.

'Stabbed,' Ylva said. 'Right here.' She opened his cloak to show her.

The woman immediately removed the scarf Ylva had used to cover the injury. She gently touched the skin close to the wound then looked up at Ylva. 'You're a Dane – did you do this? Did you hurt him?'

'No.'

'What about Cathryn?'

'She died.'

'Leave us.' The woman closed her eyes and took a deep breath to compose herself.

'You have to help him. Please, he—'

'Leave us.'

So Ylva left her with Bron, and returned to the main hall.

The building was bigger and stronger than anything Ylva had seen before. Its ceiling was so high she had to put her head back to see the cracked and faded paintings that covered it. The grey stone floor was strewn with skins and furs to make it warmer and more homely, and the walls were decorated with a collection of tapestries. Arranged around a central firepit, there were five long tables with benches either side that would each seat as many as eight people.

'Come here.' The old woman was taking a steaming pot from the fire. 'Come.'

'Are you the Witch?' Ylva asked. 'You need to help Bron.'

'Such a strong girl.' The old woman held the pot in one wrinkled hand and reached out for Ylva with the other. Her nails were thick and hard. Her knuckles were swollen and gnarled.

When Ylva recoiled, the old woman waggled her fingers, making it clear she wanted Ylva to take her hand.

'No.' Ylva stepped back.

The old woman thrust her hand closer, so Ylva put her own behind her back and shook her head. 'What's the matter with you?' Ylva asked. 'Why don't you get in there and—'

The old woman put down the pot and grabbed Ylva's wrist to pull her hand from behind her back. 'You're strong,' she said. 'You've come far. But you're not as alone as you think.'

Ylva snatched her hand away and glared at the woman. 'You're the Witch,' she said. 'You need to help Bron.'

'Do I look like a witch?'

'Yes.'

The old woman chuckled. It was a rattling, guttural sound that turned into a cough. 'Well, child, looks can be deceiving. Things aren't always as you think. My daughter Mildred is the one you need. Cathryn always called her younger sister "the Witch".'

'Her sister? She's Cathryn's sister?'

'Yes. And she will do everything she can to help Bron, I promise you that.' The old woman put a cloth into

Ylva's hand and pointed at the pot. 'Take that to her; she'll need your help.'

Ylva took the pot of boiling water into the room at the back. Mildred hardly spoke, other than to tell Ylva what to do, and as they worked to save Bron's life, Ylva watched her, thinking that she didn't look like a witch at all. And there was hardly any resemblance to her sister, Cathryn, except in her eyes.

At last, Mildred wrapped Bron's wound with a cloth bandage and stepped away from the bed.

'Will he live?' Ylva asked.

'We've done everything we can,' Mildred said. 'The only thing left is to wait and to pray.' She motioned to a stool. 'Why don't you sit down and tell me who you are?'

So Ylva sat down and told her everything.

49

Home

She began with the moment she and Mother set sail from their village, and ended with the moment she saw the island. Mildred sat with her hands folded in her lap and spoke only to ask her a question or two, and when Ylva had finished recounting her saga, Mildred told her to wait, and left her alone with Bron.

Ylva sat for a long time, watching the rise and fall of Bron's chest, and when Cathryn's sister finally returned she asked her, 'What is this place? Who are you people? I've seen only women. Shield-maidens.'

'Does that frighten you?'

Ylva thought about how strong Cathryn had been, and how she had protected her. 'No. It feels safe.'

'Good. Now, I know you must have many questions,'

Mildred said, 'and I promise I will answer them all in time, but first I want you to come with me. There are some people you should meet.'

When they returned to the main hall, there were children sitting at three of the tables. At least twenty boys and girls of all ages, sitting in silence, faces turned towards Ylva.

'This island is a safe place,' Mildred said. 'And these are all the children Cathryn has brought to us. Children who were taken as slaves, but freed by Cathryn.'

And suddenly it made sense. Ylva hadn't wanted to believe the three-fingered man when he told her that Cathryn and Bron stole slaves to sell them, but now she knew it wasn't true. They had rescued them. They had saved them not stolen them. That was something she could believe. That made sense.

'Cathryn wanted to fill every seat at every table we have,' Mildred said. 'And there's a seat for you if you want it. You're safe, Ylva. This is your home now.'

Safe, Geri whispered.

And finally, it was the right time for tears.

Glossary

All-Father – Odin, the supreme god in Norse mythology.

Bearded Axe – Also known as a 'skeggox'. The 'beard' of this type of axe is the lower part of the cutting edge that extends below the main width of the blade to provide a longer edge. The beard of the axe was used to hook an enemy's weapon and pull it out of their grasp, or to hook over a shield and pull it downwards.

Beck – A brook or stream with a stony bed. 'Beck' is commonly used in northern England, and derives from the Old Norse word 'bekkr'.

Berserker – A warrior who was said to wear a bearskin into battle. People believed that the spirits of bears possessed these warriors and gave them great strength.

Draugr (plural draugar) – An animated corpse that guards treasure, or wreaks vengeance on those who have done them wrong in life. They are horrible to look at and have superhuman strength.

Fenrir – The giant wolf that is one of the children of Loki and the giantess Angrboda. In Norse mythology, Fenrir is chained up by the gods but is destined to break his chains and fight Thor at the time of Ragnarök.

Fimbulvetr – Three years of terrible winter that will come before Ragnarök.

Freki – One of the two wolves that accompanies the god Odin. The wolves sit beside Odin at his feasting table and eat the food he throws to them. The other wolf is called Geri. Some believed that all wolves were descended from Geri and Freki.

Freya – The goddess of love and fertility, who sits in the great hall Sessrumnir. She is said to weep tears of gold.

Gaut – A person from Gautland.

Gautland – An area in the south of what is now known as Sweden.

Geirrod – A giant who tried to kill Thor by making Loki bring Thor to his castle without his magic belt and hammer.

Geri – One of the two wolves that accompanies the god Odin. The wolves sit beside Odin at his feasting table and eat the food he throws to them. The other wolf is called Freki. Some believed that all wolves were descended from Geri and Freki.

Great Heathen Army – Also known as the Great Viking Army, this was created when Norse warriors who usually fought in smaller raiding groups came together to form a single army. Made up of fighters mainly from Denmark, Sweden and Norway, the army invaded England in AD 865. Legend has it that the army was led by the sons of Ragnar Lothbrok.

Hel – The daughter of Loki, she is half-alive and half-dead. She rules over the realm of the dead, which is also called 'Hel'.

Huginn – One of Odin's two ravens that flies over Midgard and brings news. The other is called Muninn.

Idun – The Norse goddess who owns and guards the golden apples that give eternal youth and immortality.

Idun's Apples – The golden apples of youth. Eating the apples keeps the Norse gods young and healthy.

Jarl – A Norse or Danish chieftain often in control of a village. Jarls were second in importance to the king.

Jormungandr – The giant serpent that is, according to the legends, one of the children of Loki and the giantess Angrboda. Also known as the Midgard Serpent or the World Serpent, Jormungandr is said to circle Midgard and bite on his own tail.

Kohl – An ancient eye cosmetic often used to darken the area around the eyes.

Loki – The mischief-making god.

Mare – An evil spirit that sits on a person's chest and gives them nightmares while they are sleeping.

Midgard – One of the nine realms of Norse mythology, Midgard is the middle world, the world of men.

Muninn – One of Odin's two ravens that flies over Midgard and brings news. The other is called Huginn.

Niflheim – One of the nine realms of Norse mythology, Niflheim is the realm of cold, mist and darkness.

Norns – The three goddesses who, according to Norse mythology, spin the fates of all creatures, including the gods. Viking warriors fought bravely in battle because they believed their fate had already been decided by the Norns.

Odin – The supreme god in Norse mythology, who sits in the great hall Valhalla.

Ragnar Lothbrok (or Lodbrok) – A popular Norse hero and legendary Viking warrior. His name means Ragnar 'Hairy Breeches', and he was so-called because he wore hairy animal-skin trousers.

Ragnarök – The final, apocalyptic battle involving all creation, in which almost all life will be destroyed.

Saga – Story.

Skald – A person who told poems and sagas, and recited them at feasts and gatherings to honour great heroes and their brave deeds.

Sleipnir – Odin's eight-legged horse.

Thor – The son of Odin, Thor is the thunder god. He is the second most important god in Norse mythology, and is seen as the keeper of law and order. While warriors prayed to Odin, the common people prayed to Thor.

Thrall – Slave.

Tine River – The River Tyne.

Ulfhednar – Warriors who were said to wear wolfskins into battle. People believed that the spirits of wolves possessed these warriors and gave them special powers.

Valhalla – A huge hall watched over by Odin, where dead warriors fight and feast as they await Ragnarök.

Valkyries – Young women who collect warriors killed on the battlefield and take them to Valhalla.

Yggdrasil – Sometimes called the World Tree, this is the mythical ash tree that links all nine realms of Norse mythology.

Did You Know?

The Viking Age is usually said to have lasted between the years 793 and 1066.

The first significant Viking raid in England was in the year 793 at Lindisfarne, close to the part of England where Ylva's story takes place. But experts believe that Vikings had raided England at least once before, in Portsmouth, four years earlier.

Experts can't be sure that anyone ever actually called the raiders 'Vikings', and there's a lot of debate about where the word even came from. Records suggest it became a popular word long after the Viking Age was over. It's more likely that the raiders who came across the North Sea were known simply as 'Danes', 'Norsemen' or 'Northmen'.

Vikings did not wear horned helmets. In fact, most of them probably didn't even wear helmets at all. Swords and helmets were extremely expensive and difficult to make, so those who did own them were usually either very rich, or had taken them from an enemy they defeated in battle. An axe, like the one Ylva uses to fight the bear, was much more common because it was cheap and easy to make, and it could be used both as a weapon and as an everyday tool.

Experts know that Old Norse, as spoken by the Vikings, and Old English, as spoken by the Anglo-

Saxons, were very similar languages because many of the original Anglo-Saxon settlers came from Scandinavia – the home of the Vikings. Anglo-Saxons, like Cathryn and Bron, would have thought the invading Vikings had strange accents, but they would have understood what they were saying.

Murder was a serious crime in Viking culture, and revenge was hugely important. If a person was killed fairly in battle that was fine, but murder had to be punished. That's why Ylva is so determined to avenge Mother's death. But sometimes a single murder could lead to a long and bloody string of revenge killings.

Slaves like Ylva were the least important people in Viking culture. They were seen as cattle, and the law did not recognize them as humans. Slaves were not allowed to own property, they were not allowed to marry, and their children automatically belonged to their owners. Slaves were often treated badly, and were forced to carry out the most difficult and unpleasant tasks in the home and farm. A man who killed or stole another man's slave would have to pay the owner as if he had killed that man's cow or pig, or stolen his property.

If a slave owner died, his slaves were often sacrificed and buried with him.

Slaves were one of the most common trade items in Viking culture, so they were extremely valuable to raiders – like the three-fingered man – who captured and sold them. Vikings brought slaves back from their raids overseas, but they also enslaved people from their own countries.

Some historians think that the Great Heathen Army

attacked Eoforwic (York) on 1st November 866 (the month before Ylva arrived in England). This was already a time of civil war in the kingdom of Northumbria, with the two Saxons kings – Aelle and Osbert – fighting for control.

When Vikings took control of Eoforwic, they changed its name to Jorvik, but the city is now known as York.

It's difficult to be certain of many of the dates and facts about the Vikings during the time of Ylva's adventure, because the Vikings didn't write their sagas and histories down at that time. A lot of information was passed by word of mouth, and not actually written until many years later, and by that time some of the facts were either forgotten or changed. Most written records of the time come from other people writing about the Vikings. For instance, much of the information we have about the Great Heathen Army comes from the *Anglo-Saxon Chronicle*, but it doesn't give us very much detail. Historians are unsure exactly who led the army, when it arrived, how big it was, or why the warriors came. According to the saga *The Tale of Ragnar's Sons*, the army came to avenge the death of Ragnar Lothbrok, a famous Viking adventurer and warrior, who was thrown into a pit of snakes by King Aella of Northumbria. The army was said to have been led by Ragnar's sons, who included Ivar the Boneless, Halfdan Ragnarsson, Hvitserk Ragnarsson, Bjorn Ironside, and Sigurd Snake-in-the-Eye. Other stories and sources suggest they were joined by the Viking chieftans known as Guthrum and Ubba (who might also have been a son of Ragnar Lothbrok).

Acknowledgements

I've learnt a lot about Vikings while writing this book. I've also realized there's still so much more for me to learn. But what's *really* amazing is how much we just don't know – and probably never will know – about the Viking age. In a way, that made life difficult for me when trying to find information for my story, but in the end it worked out for the best because it allowed me to use my imagination to fill in the gaps. I am, after all, a story-teller, not a historian. And being a storyteller means I could put mountains where there are none, and I could make Ylva battle a bear even though the last bears probably died out in England about 100 years before Ylva's ship ever reached these shores.

So it turns out that I've learnt something about bears as well as Vikings.

When I see Ylva's story on these pages, as you have just done, it feels strange to think that it didn't come to me fully formed. But that's the way of stories; they develop and evolve until they become what they need to be – and sometimes the only way to find the heart of a story is to discuss it with other story-lovers, and to listen to their ideas. Well, lucky for me, I had Barry Cunningham right there at the beginning to help Ylva on her way, so thank you Barry, you have an excellent nose for sniffing out a good story. (He also has a beard that any Viking would be proud of, but don't tell him I said that.)

Thank you also to Rachel Hickman, who was there to offer ideas and encouragement. Your enthusiasm confirmed that this was the right story to tell, and you later commissioned talented artist Jill Calder to design the eye-catching and unique illustration that looks so amazing on the cover of *She Wolf*.

When it comes to the nitty-gritty of the story, though, it was Rachel Leyshon who stood at the front of the battle with me, axe in hand. Rachel endured my persistent emails and Friday morning calls to talk through all the crazy ideas. It was also Rachel who kept saying 'Oh, there's just one more thing . . .' which usually meant *more* than just one thing and often resulted in me rewriting another section of the story. But Rachel is always, *always* upbeat, insightful (and right), and a pleasure to work with. Thank you, Rachel – you have a way of finding the truth of a story, and Ylva's quest for revenge wouldn't be what it is without your advice.

Laura, you've done an awesome job with the layouts and making sure everything looks so good inside the pages of this book – and you've had to put up with the irritation of me changing things along the way, so thank you for all your patience.

Thanks also to Elinor who I know is working hard to send *She Wolf* adventuring across the sea, which is where any true Viking would want to be. Thanks to Claire for working hard on the copy-edit, to Jazz for organizing events, publicity, and being all-round awesome, and thanks to the rest of the brilliant team at Chicken House – Kesia, Esther, Sarah and Lucy! It's a pleasure to work with you guys.

It's hard to believe that I've now been working with my agent, Ella, for over a year. Ella has lived up to all expectations – with a keen eye for a story, a love of the fine detail, and an in-depth knowledge of the Viking age! I know you're there to battle alongside me, Ella, so thank you for all your support and encouragement.

Writing books and sending them out into the world can sometimes feel like a lonely business, and I can only hope that they reach as many happy readers as possible. That can't happen without reviewers, book-lovers and booksellers who enjoy my books and recommend them to their friends, readers and customers. There are a few special people who have championed my books for a long time now, so I want to say a huge thank you to them too – with a special mention for Helen at Forum Books, Fiona at Waterstones, Richard at Drake, and Sharleene at Seven Stories.

But where would I be without my Viking clan? My shield-maiden and my warriors? (By which I mean my brilliant wife and children.) Who would I annoy? Who would I ignore when I'm lost in a story? Who would I use as a sounding board for ideas? Who would I hit with the axe that now hangs over my desk? (Don't worry, the axe is made of foam.) I couldn't do any of this without them; they're the best, and I'd go adventuring with them any time.

And lastly (did you just sigh in relief?), *and lastly*, I want to say thanks to you guys. Yes, you. The ones holding *She Wolf* right now. You are the readers tucked up in bed, or relaxing by the window, or snuggled on the sofa. You're sitting on the bus, the train, the plane. You're safe in your special place. You're in the classroom with one of those amazing teachers who loves books and stories and knows exactly how to spread that love (you teachers are awesome, by the way). You are a reader. Be proud of that. Stories make us better people; they take us to new places and they show us amazing things. An immeasurable amount of good comes from reading, but that's not the best reason to pick up a book. Nope. The best reason to pick up a book is because stories are fun. And who doesn't want to have fun?

MY FRIEND THE ENEMY

1941. It's wartime and when a German plane crashes in flames near Peter's home, he rushes over hoping to find something exciting to keep.

But what he finds instead is an injured young airman. He needs help, but can either of them trust the enemy?

. . . an exciting, thought-provoking book.
THE BOOKSELLER

Paperback, ISBN 978-1-912626-35-9, £6.99 • ebook, ISBN 978-1-909489-06-6, £6.99

BELOW ZERO

When Zak's plane crash-lands on Outpost Zero, a small Antarctic research base in one of the most isolated places on Earth, he discovers a cold, dark nightmare. The power's out and the people who live there have disappeared. Worse, as he searches for answers, bizarre visions suggest a link to something else – deep beneath the ice – which only he can understand . . .

Paperback, ISBN 978-1-910655-92-4, £6.99 • ebook, ISBN 978-1-911077-55-8, £6.99

BOY X

Kidnapped, Ash McCarthy wakes up on a remote tropical island. Why is he there? And how can he get home? Ash needs answers.

To escape, he must take risks. But what's more dangerous: the jungle, his captors, or the chemical injected in his veins?

Boy X is a breathless adventure where nothing and no-one is expected. Dan Smith's pacey prose gallops along, capturing the reader and entangling us in the puzzle plot.
THE SCOTSMAN

Paperback, ISBN 978-1-909489-04-2, £6.99 • ebook, ISBN 978-1-910655-52-8, £6.99

MY BROTHER'S SECRET

Twelve-year-old Karl is a good German boy. He wants his country to win the war – after all, his father has gone away to fight. But when tragedy strikes and his older brother Stefan gets into trouble, he begins to lose his faith in Hitler. Before long, he's caught up in a deadly rebellion.

Rich in detail, this is a thought-provoking story.

JULIA ECCLESHARE

Paperback, ISBN 978-1-909489-03-5, £6.99 • ebook, ISBN 978-1-909489-54-7, £6.99